PA
A Collection
NO
of
RA
Short Stories
MA

notionpress.com

PANORAMA

A Collection of Short Stories

Shilpi Chaklanobis

notionpress.com

Notion Press

Old No. 38, New No. 6
McNichols Road, Chetpet
Chennai - 600 031

First Published by Notion Press 2016

ISBN 978-93-5206-966-8

Dedication

This book is dedicated to my parents, Late Smt. Bani Chaklanobis and Late Sri. Birendra Nath Chaklanobis, who have always showered me with their selfless love without asking for anything in return.

Contents

Acknowledgements

First and foremost I would like to thank God for making me capable enough to write this book. I would also like to express my gratitude to many people who saw me through this book:

My elder sister, Dr Sujata Chaklanobis for being there for me and always believing in my dreams. Her constant encouragement has made it possible for me to churn out this book.

My eldest sister, Mrs Sumita C Banerjee, brothers-in-law, Dr S. P. Banerjee and Mr I. Chakraborty and my niece Mitali for encouraging me at every step of my life. A special thanks to my darling niece Priya for giving her honest feedback on my written pieces that helped me evolve as a writer.

Gulzar Sahab for being a constant source of inspiration.

Dr Sanjay Wadhawan for his exemplary support and inspiring me to write this book.

I would also like to thank the myriad authors who have given me my passion for books.

The entire team of Notion Press for giving wings to my imagination.

And my sincere thanks to the readers for picking up and reading this book.

Story 1: Wok

Rani folded the chapatti (bread) into a roll, dipped it in hot tea and put it into her mouth.

"Don't go out in the sun to play when I am not around. Go to Poonam Kaki's house and play with Meena," Vimala said while tying her hair into a braid, but Rani's whole attention was on her breakfast. She was sitting on the floor at the center of the small ten by ten room, enjoying every bit of her breakfast.

Wiping the drops of tea with her hand that had rolled down her chin, Rani finished the remaining portion of the *chapatti*, picked up the cup with both her hands and emptied it into her mouth ensuring not a single drop of tea is left behind. Staring back at the empty cup she called, "Amma."

"Hmm?" Vimala, who was now arranging the plates of her bright orange polyester sari, said casually. She arranged her *pallu* and prevented it from dropping off her shoulder, pinning it with a safety pin.

"Why don't you make potato curry with roti?"

"Because we don't have a wok *beta*. I had told you the other day," Vimala fumbled for a moment but quickly controlled her emotions and responded to Rani's innocent query.

"Poonam Kaki makes potato curry every day. I had tasted it once. It was so yummy," Rani's eyes gleamed with the thought of the delicious potato curry. "This big potato pieces in yellow curry tasted so nice, I still remember the taste," she joyfully said, displaying the size of potato pieces in the curry with her tiny hands.

"Okay, I'll also make potato curry for you when I buy a wok," Vimala said and came to Rani. Sitting on her knees she hugged Rani to her chest and kissed her head. Rani's face started glowing with the mere thought of having *chapattis* with potato curry one day, when her Amma will be able to manage enough money to buy a wok.

Still wandering in the world of vegetables and curries, Rani exclaimed suddenly with the thought of tasting a new vegetable, "And eggplant also. They look so beautiful. Must be very tasty also. Okay?" But amidst all this excitement she couldn't notice small drops of tears shining at the corner of Vimala's eyes.

"All right. Eggplant also," Vimala said with a feeble smile and got up to leave.

"And lady fingers, pumpkins, cauliflowers…," Rani, who was still sitting on the floor, repeated names of all the vegetables she could remember like the tables of two, rocking back and forth. Leaving her day dreaming about different types of vegetable curries, Vimala bent and rolled her hands on Rani's head, kissed her cheeks and left for work after putting on her slippers hurriedly.

Being a Sunday morning, the roads were comparatively empty. "It's already 6:45 am. Bhabhi must be very angry," Vimala thought and increased her pace, dreading a scolding for being late. Usually she reaches Shanta's house that is located in the posh locality of the city by six-thirty in the morning. She has been working there as a domestic help since many years and could not afford to lose the job. With trembling hands, she put her fingers on the doorbell and pressed it.

"Why so late? See it's already seven!" Shanta frowned while opening the door.

"I am so sorry Bhabhi. Could not get up early in the morning. Rani kept me awake till late night," she said and quickly went inside the kitchen to wash the utensils.

"Why don't you put Rani into school? She is almost six now," Shanta came behind her and asked while she was preparing the tea.

"It's so difficult to make ends meet with the small amount I earn by working in these houses. And now with such a big loan on my head after Rani's father's death… how will I pay her fees?" she said taking a deep breath while she cleaned the utensils with a scrub.

"But the municipal schools teach free of cost. It's not right to keep her illiterate."

"And what about books, uniforms? From where I will arrange those?"

"Okay, you admit her in the school. I'll see what I can do for her," Shanta said pouring the tea into three cups. She took out two biscuits from the box and handed them over to Vimala with a cup of tea. Shanta always felt a connection with the poor little girl. Rani was only six months old when Vimala had started working in her house. Shanta had seen her growing every bit and felt a concern from deep within.

After she finished washing the utensils, Vimala came to the hall where Shanta and Rohit, her husband, were having their morning tea. Both of them were reading the newspaper after finishing the tea and the empty cups were lying on the table.

"Bhabhi, do you have some leftover curry in the fridge?" Vimala asked with much apprehension.

Shanta lifted her eyes from the newspaper and asked, "Why?"

"Rani is very keen to have *chapattis* with curry. So I thought if you have some leftovers in the fridge, she can have it today during lunch."

"Don't you make curries? What do you have with *chapattis* then?" Shanta, hit by sudden shock and surprise, counter-questioned her.

"Sometimes with pickle and sometimes I prepare *dal*. But *dal* has also become so expensive. God knows how people like us will survive," Vimala sighed.

"All right. I'll give you the curry that I will make today. Take it for both of you," Shanta said.

Vimala's eyes glowed after hearing Shanta's words and a look of immense satisfaction covered her face with the thought of fulfilling Rani's wish at least for a day. It seemed to her that she was filled with an unknown energy, and quickly collected the empty cups from the table to wash.

Shanta had always been very soft hearted, with a strong empathy for people like Vimala. She had seen Rani from her infancy and her heart pined for this tiny soul who was leading a cursed life of poverty and deprivation for no fault of hers. It was God who had sent her in a family where eating *chapatti* with curry was also being considered as a luxury. This huge disparity in the society stirred her soul and she felt restless to do something for them. That day she specially prepared *matar paneer* to please the kid. She wanted to give Rani a few moments in life that she could cherish.

"Take this for Rani and tell me how she liked it," Shanta said while handing over the box full of *matar paneer* to Vimala.

Shanta's little gesture appeared like an oasis in her life that had become like a cactus in the burning desert. Thanking her from the bottom of her heart, Vimala took the box.

It was late noon by the time Vimala finished the morning shift work. She wiped the small beads of sweat from her forehead and looked up at the sky. The sun was shining with all its might. Unable to bear the heat, she rushed towards her home to reach as quickly as possible. Rani, who was playing with Meena, came running and hugged Vimala when she saw her coming. Spotting the small steel box in Vimala's hand she asked

"What is this Amma?"

"It's a surprise for you," Vimala said, smiling. "Show me. I want to see."

"Come," Vimala said and took Rani inside the house, holding her little fingers with one hand and the box in the other. She served herself and Rani the *chapattis* that she had already prepared in the morning, poured the curry in Rani's plate and took out a piece of mango pickle for herself from the jar. Rani's eyes twinkled with joy when she saw the fluffy and juicy square *paneer* pieces peeking from the creamy curry and green round peas.

"We'll have curry today," Rani's heart leapt with joy and she started clapping.

"Okay, now be a good girl and finish your food," Vimala said, beholding Rani's innocent face with affection. Needless to say Rani had already started gulping, making large morsels of the food. Vimala kept on gazing at Rani with her eyes gleaming with contentment and affection, while tears rolled down her cheeks.

The joy of festivity had filled the whole atmosphere. The clear blue autumn sky, the dazzling sunshine, the fragrance of *parijat* flowers, all seemed to be celebrating the advent of Dussehra. A huge statue of Ravana was placed at the center stage of the Ramlila ground where stalls were getting ready to welcome the ten days of celebration. Vendors from far and near had come to sell items of various kinds and were busy decorating their shops to lure their customers. Everywhere there was happiness and laughter of people enjoying the autumn celebration. Everyone was eager to go to the fair and enjoy with friends and family. The stage for Ramlila had already been set and people were waiting eagerly to watch the story of Lord Rama, which was being enacted by a well-known drama company.

"Amma, I want to go to the fair," Rani said pulling Vimala's *pallu*. All her friends were planning to go there and she also didn't want to miss the fun. Vimala was finishing the household chores quickly as she had to leave for work. Every house where she worked had loads of cleaning and other odd jobs waiting for her because of the upcoming festival. Vimala had to put extra hours to meet the demands of all her employers.

"How can I take you there *beta*? In every house I have to put extra hours to manage the extra workload."

"But I want to see the Ravana and ride the giant wheel also," Rani said and started crying rubbing her eyes with the fists.

Vimala felt as if someone is squeezing her heart. Poverty is like a leech. It doesn't kill you, but sucks your blood to the extent that you stop living. She had never felt so helpless when she cannot even fulfil such a petty wish of her darling daughter. After the death of her husband, she had to manage everything–from home to earning their livelihood. And among all this chaos, Rani was suffering the most, her childhood lost in the poverty they were living in.

Perplexed with Rani's crying, Vimala tried to calm her down, "Okay, I'll try." She wiped her tears, making Rani sit on her lap and said, "Now wipe off these tears. You look awful while crying." Vimala tried to laugh. For the moment she calmed Rani down but the thought kept her troubling throughout the day. That day, her mind kept wandering about the means and ways to arrange some money to take Rani to the fair. During these six years, she had not been able to provide her even the basic necessities of life. Her heart bled when she watched kids of her age going to school, hanging school bags on their shoulders. She had not bought a single dress for Rani for the past two years and was managing with the old dresses that she got from her employers. She wanted her child to bloom and would do anything to fill her life with happiness.

In the evening, the sun was setting and the light outside was becoming dull with every passing moment. The birds rustled and chattered as they settled down to sleep. Vimala, exhausted with the entire day's work, wanted to fly home after the long tiring day and be with her daughter who was alone since morning. She was quickly moving her hands to finish the job but her heart sank when Shanta called her.

Slowly she went to Shanta and stood there, still, when it seemed that honey filled through her ears.

"Here, take this money for the extra work you have done during the past few days," Shanta took out five crisp hundred rupees notes from her wallet and handed them over to Vimala. She extended her hands to take the notes from Shanta and tied them at the corner of her *pallu*. Next day was the last day of the festivity and there was still a chance for Rani to enjoy the fair. She felt a fresh breath of air fill her lungs at the thought of sending Rani to the fair and giving her a day where Rani could evade the shackles of poverty and get the childhood she deserved. She would not be able to take Rani herself due to her job, but at least she could send her with Meena and other children from the neighbourhood.

When she reached home, it was dark everywhere. She could see the dim hazy lights coming from the houses in the locality where she lived. Rani was dozing when she reached home. Taking her into her lap, she kissed her and said, "I have a surprise for you!"

"Curry?" asked Rani, rubbing her sleepy eyes with her hands, but her voice was full of excitement.

"No, better than that," Vimala said.

"Show me?" Rani got up and sat by her side, stretching her tiny hands in front of Vimala's face. Vimala took out a hundred-rupee note and placed it in Rani's hand. Rani's eyes widened. She felt as if someone had opened the doors of a treasury for her. She couldn't believe her eyes. Hundred rupees were resting on her palm. With this treasure she could buy countless things–toys, sweets, doll, *chaat* and what not. She was feeling ecstatic with the thought of going to the fair and buying things that were otherwise like a distant dream for her.

"Tomorrow, go with Meena and other friends to the fair."

"And you Amma?" she asked observing the note curiously by turning it from both the sides.

"I can't come *beta*. I have work. By the time I will get back home, everything will be over."

For a moment a certain disappointment engulfed Rani but soon the joy of visiting the fair and buying new things brushed all her sadness away.

"Keep this money carefully with you and spend it wisely," Vimala instructed her.

"Don't worry, Amma. I am a big girl now. Don't I stay alone like a good girl when you are out at work?"

"Yes, I know my darling," Vimala said caressing her head. "That is why I am saying, don't be mischievous. Be with Meena and other friends else you will be lost in the fair."

Rani spent the whole night watching the ceiling while lying beside Vimala. She kept daydreaming about the things she would buy tomorrow. Only when the morning rays started appearing in the sky in an orange-yellow shade and the birds started chirping, her eyes closed and she managed to get some sleep.

Vimala dusted the trunk and took out the dress Shanta had given for Rani last year. This was the dress that Rani wore during special occasions. Rani gave a cry of joy when she looked at herself in the mirror wearing the lovely red frock with prints of flowers. Vimala combed her hair and put on a red beaded necklace.

When Rani left for the fair with her friends, she felt like the richest person on the earth. She had one hundred rupees with her and she could buy the world with it. The path seemed endless while walking to the Ramlila ground and when she saw it, Rani started running quickly. The huge giant wheel was visible even from outside the gate. Many vendors were selling balloons, masks, toys etc. and had occupied the entrance of the gate attracting their potential customers by displaying various items that they were selling. Everywhere there was a bustle of people enjoying the colourful fair.

Meena bought one toy watch for herself. It was very nice with large digits printed on it. For a moment Rani got tempted but the next moment she thought, "What will I do with it? I don't go out to work and I can't read either." She moved away from the stall towards the entrance. Holding her head high like an empress and clasping her palms together behind her back, she entered the Ramlila ground. The first thing that caught her attention was the huge statue of Ravana. Everywhere there were people enjoying the rides, playing games, eating their favourite foods and making merry. On the right, one shop was selling various types of sweets. *Barfi, jalebi, imarti, laddoo*–there were so many varieties kept in huge piles that it became difficult for her to choose her favourite one. Rani walked towards the shop mesmerised by the bright orange colour of the large juicy *imarti*.

"Kaka, what is this sweet called?" she asked the shopkeeper.

"*Imarti.*"

"How much does it cost?"

"Ten rupees for two."

"Ten rupees for two? My God!" Rani thought and started calculating on her fingers the amount she will be left with after buying the *imarti*.

"No, these don't seem to be tasty enough," she told herself and headed towards another shop that was selling toys while comparing the sweetness of two *imartis* with a ten rupee note in her mind.

The toyshop had all kinds of toys, stuffed toys, kitchen sets, dolls, plastic pistols and what not. A sudden smile came to her face when she picked a doll from the stall that wore a beautiful pink dress and had blue eyes that blinked.

"What is the cost of this doll?" she asked the shopkeeper. "Fifty rupees," the shopkeeper replied.

"Fifty?" her eyes widened as if she has seen a ghost. Scared with the thought of losing half of her treasure in the bargain, Rani left the shop and stepped ahead. She scanned one shop after another to find the most appropriate thing that she could buy with the precious hundred rupees that rested in her pocket.

She was watching the shooting game when her eyes sparkled after spotting one shop at the corner of the ground. She rushed to the shop and picked up a wok that the shop was selling.

"How much Kaka?"

"Hundred rupees," the shopkeeper replied.

Rani felt as if someone has crushed her heart ruthlessly. Buying the wok would mean she won't be able to have even a candy for herself. She had been dreaming the whole night about the things she would buy from the fair, but after buying this wok she wouldn't be left with any money to purchase a single thing from the list she had prepared in her mind. But the next moment her thoughts were taken over by the tastes of all those delicacies that she has only heard of, but never tasted. Without a wok, it was impossible to taste those heavenly dishes. After thinking for a couple of moments, she took out the hundred-rupee note from her pocket and picked the wok. Unable to stay there for a moment, she rushed home to show Amma what she had got from the fair.

Vimala had returned from work and was waiting for Rani at the doorstep when she saw her coming towards her, running. She heaved a sigh of relief and happiness after seeing Rani happy and content, unaware of the fact that what havoc the next moment will wreck on her. Rani came to Vimala with both her hands behind her and said, "Amma, sit down and close your eyes." Vimala could feel something heavy being dropped into her lap.

"Now open them."

Slowly Vimala opened her eyes and put her hand on her head in dismay.

"What is this?"

"See Amma, you don't even know! This is a wok," Rani said, amused at the thought that Vimala didn't recognize a wok.

"But why did you get a wok?" Vimala asked with shaking voice.

"Because you didn't have one to cook curry," she said innocently.

"But I had given you the money to have fun. To buy toys and sweets for yourself," Vimala said, shocked.

"So what? Now that we have a wok, I can have potato curry with *roti* that you will cook for me every day. Won't you Amma?" Rani asked innocently brimming with joy. Unable to answer her question, Vimala kept on staring at her innocent face with wet eyes, softly running her hands through Rani's hair. She didn't realise when tears started flowing from her eyes.

When Rani fell asleep, Vimala, with a heavy heart, took the wok and locked it in the almirah where another wok was lying quietly. She looked at the twin woks mocking her, with a stream of tears flowing down her cheeks. Now she would have to invent another valid excuse for Rani to explain why she couldn't prepare potato curry for her.

Story 2: Peanut

What should I say about him? His silky hair that reminds me of the finest silk from Arab, his twinkling eyes that can even beat the sparkle of the Kohinoor enjoying royal status in the Queen's land or his loving hug that is simply unmatched in the world?

Words fail when I try to describe him. All I can say about him is: he is the one who has been my friend since the day I arrived in this world. He had always been around, playing with me, being mischievous and always taking care of me. He imitated everything that I did, whether it was watching a cartoon show on the TV or running after butterflies in the park. One thing that both of us loved doing together was listening to a famous kids' song in Bengali. Well I am not fully sure how much he enjoyed the song, but have always found him following me to listen to it whenever Baba played the record for me. He used to jump on the chair beside me and quietly stare at the record revolving over the spools. At times he used to steal a glance at me and again start watching the record moving on the player.

Kuchkuche Kalo She Jaate Spaniel

Tultule Ga Jeno Reshami Rumal

Ami Take Pushipol Nam Die Daki

Pushipol E Shohore Ache Ektai

Pushipol Pushipol Tumi Je Amar

Pushipol Pushipol Amio Tomar

Dujone Te Khela Kori

Dujone Berai

Pushipol E Shohore Ache Ektai

He's so pitch-black Spaniel breed dog

His coat is like silk handkerchief

I call him by the name Pushipol

There is only one Pushipol in this town

Pushipol Pushipol you are mine

Pushipol Pushipol I am also yours

The duo are both on the move

Playing on the streets

There is only one Pushipol in this town

The song made me forget the world around me and I could spend hours listening to it with Peanut. Every word of the song reminded me of the special bond that Peanut and I shared. So what if my little Pomeranian was not pitch-black? With silky white coat of fur and twinkling eyes, my Peanut was the most beautiful dog in the world. Peanut had come into this house and my father's life much before I became a part of it. Baba had brought him home when he was a little puppy, merely a day old. He was Peanut's first friend not only in this house but also in this world. As far as I am concerned, I was first a competitor for him who had come to disturb his friendship with Baba. But later on he gladly accepted me as his friend and now we, the duo, were the best friends ever.

There is a very interesting story behind naming him Peanut. It was a dark winter evening when he first landed in my father's lap. Baba, while walking home through the cold, dark lanes while carrying little Peanut in his arms, protecting him from the chilly breeze, was struggling to find a suitable name for him. Suddenly his attention was drawn by a vendor who passed by him selling large fluffy peanuts. "Peanut"–almost instantly the name flashed in his mind. "Yes, I will call him Peanut," he thought. Cute, adorable and loved by everyone.

Since the day I started recognising people, I have seen him around. As I said earlier he considered me to be his competitor but this never discouraged him to quietly love me. But later we had the best time ever when he accepted me fully in his life. I loved to play in the park in front of my house with him but I had to earn it. Ma allowed us to go out to play only when she was assured that I had finished my homework. And while I completed it, Peanut used to wait very patiently, sitting in front of me, looking at me with his shiny black eyes.

He was also my companion and secret-keeper in the mischief that I did. Whenever Ma used to prepare my favourite sweet dish and keep it out of my reach to save the poor sweet to be gulped in a single day, it was Peanut's job to locate the hideout of the special dish for me and bring me the report of a clear path to my target. We would both tiptoe to the hideout while Ma took a short nap in the afternoon and gobble down a good portion of the sweet in a single sitting. Later when Ma would find out about our great achievement, he would also share the scolding showered on me, standing quietly beside me with his head bowed down.

But in the midst of all this, the person he adored and loved the most was Baba. Like the discovery of his name, Peanut's entry into Baba's life was also very dramatic. It was Baba's first job in Delhi and he felt extremely happy when the brown envelope with the government seal landed on his hand. Bursting with happiness and eyes full of dreams of a beautiful life ahead, Baba came to Delhi to start his new journey in the land of opportunities. But everything in life comes with a price tag. The cut-throat competition to reach the top and ever increasing work pressures to meet the tight deadlines can sometimes drain you to the extent that you feel like screaming from the top of a mountain to let you live in peace. When you are constantly surrounded by a million people, screaming, shouting, wanting to be heard, the need for a loving caring companion is felt the most.

Born and brought up in a joint family, Baba had been trying hard to cope with the new challenges and going through a million emotions when Peanut arrived like a boon in his life. November was about to end and the chill in the atmosphere had been increasing with every passing day.

Delhi's winters are terrible. There are people who think otherwise but I don't see any romance in going to India Gate at midnight for enjoying ice creams. What is the fun in gulping down frozen dessert when I am frozen to the core myself? Even today I am still trying to figure out what is so spectacular about strolling on the streets of Rajpath at midnight while shivering so hard that you feel like your teeth are going to fall off?

So, on one such winter night, the phone shrieked like a siren when Baba was busy doing his latest assignment. The phone ring echoed in the pin-drop silence of the room as all of his colleagues had left for the day. The sound made him jump over his seat and after a good thirty seconds, he was able to comprehend the situation. Wondering who could be calling at this hour, Baba picked the receiver.

"Hello," he said.

"My Bella has given birth to five cute puppies. Would you like to take one?" an excited voice of one of his friends came from the other end.

Rejoiced at the idea of coming back home with someone to greet and meet him, Baba agreed instantaneously. Winding up the tasks quickly, he reached his friend's house, and five cute puppies lying on a blanket welcomed him. Gently, he picked Peanut, the cutest one among them, a teardrop escaping his eyes. It was as tiny as a tennis ball, soft as candyfloss, unable to even open his eyes. Baba had felt as if the Maharaja of some estate had voluntarily opened his treasury for him. He caressed Peanut with his fingers when it tried to open its eyes to glance at his new owner, making a meek sound like a squeaky toy. Perhaps that was the moment when both of them were bound in an eternal bond of friendship, making a silent promise with each other to be together and protect each other for times to come.

For the next few days, Baba would forget the world around him except for shopping for his new friend. His eyes would scan all through the shops to choose the best things for Peanut, without any intention of settling for the second best. And what a shopping it was! Along with the special status in Baba's heart, Peanut had been also enjoying the things he got - a new bed, a rug, a mattress, a special chair… the list was endless.

While arranging for a comfortable home for Peanut, Baba had not realised what a daunting task awaited him. Struggling hard with the pains of raising a new born, Baba got frequent spells of sweating beneath several layers of warm clothes. Peanut was too small to hold the nipple of the feeding bottle and so a cotton ball replaced it to move the milk from the bowl to his mouth. Many such challenging situations occurred while raising Peanut but Baba overcame every hurdle, becoming an expert in raising little puppies.

Peanut was one year old when Ma came into Baba's and his life. Adorning every photograph of their wedding with his gracious presence, Peanut ensured he was at Ma's side during all the rituals. Ma always talks about her first day as a bride in the house when Peanut kept on running around her, jumping and wagging his tail. She was the new bride and Peanut had the full right, more than anyone else, to welcome and show his affection for her.

Ma had also accepted him gladly in her life. She still remembers how he started jumping when he sensed Baba's arrival after a long day's work. With the inborn talent of recognising people with their smell from a distance, he would jump and run to the front gate as soon as he smelled Baba's return from his office. He never missed welcoming and greeting Baba at the gate in the evening. The incentive? Baba's hug and loving hand caressing his head.

Following the path shown by my predecessor, I also started following Peanut every day to welcome Baba when I started walking, stumbling, crawling and that's when Peanut saw a great competitor in me. His wait for the whole day was earlier rewarded by a loving pat and a hug by Baba. But now as soon as Baba saw me running towards him with extended arms, he rushed to me and picked me into his lap before hugging Peanut. Now that was simply unacceptable for Peanut! How could he tolerate being number two in Baba's life? So he had the full right to lie down in his cot, sulking, unless Baba came and coaxed him. Only after hours of cajoling and coaxing did he become normal again.

Peanut was a great help to Ma also. She still tells us how he used to guard the jars of pickles from birds and cats when Ma left them out in the sun to mature. He used to sit by the side of the jars throughout the afternoon and relaxed only after driving the cat out of the fence whenever he saw one. This is the reason why Ma always gave some credit to Peanut by patting his head whenever we praised her for the tasty pickles.

Life was smooth and cheerful with Ma, Baba and Peanut when a sudden storm blew away everything. It was a beautiful Sunday evening when the sun was setting at the west and the clear blue sky had turned golden, shining with the radiance of the setting sun. Baba took Peanut and me out to buy me some candies when suddenly a black rabid dog came out from the bushes. Everyone was stunned with the appearance of the fierce dog that appeared to tear everyone apart with his sharp canines. He was constantly barking at us while staring with his large red eyes. Baba froze; for a moment his nerves became numb and his fist clung tight on my fingers. With one hand he was holding my fingers, with the other, Peanut's rope. Unable to decide his move, Baba was looking for a stone when Peanut, without losing a moment, jumped at the barking dog to stop him from approaching us. We shouted at the top of our voice to shoo the rabid dog but both of them were entangled with each other fighting for life. Picking up a thick stick Baba also joined Peanut to drive the dog away but it was a tough one to give up. After fighting for a good five minutes, we were able to drive the rabid dog. But these five minutes proved to be the most expensive ones that cost us immensely.

All the medicines in the world along with our love and care could not evade the inevitable. Peanut got rabies. We did not recognise this Peanut who was lying in the doctor's clinic, weak and helpless. For a moment he opened his eyes and closed them again after getting assured of Baba's presence by his side. The ever jumping Peanut did not move even a bit when the doctor pierced the needle into him.

With every passing day, he was getting a bit closer to death. Three days had passed since the incident, making him so weak that he could not even sit. Ma had made him lie in the courtyard, his favourite spot for waiting for Baba in the evening, covering him with a blanket. Her every effort to feed him even a drop of water had failed. Peanut was waiting eagerly for Baba. There was still some time left for him to come home but with every moment the wait was become even more unbearable for him.

Suddenly Ma noticed a little activity in his body and she knew Baba was coming. Baba rushed to him when he reached home and found Peanut trying to lift his head. Baba bent on his knees to lift him when their eyes exchanged looks. His pain, love, gratitude, everything had painted his eyes in a strange colour. For a moment he looked at Baba and then leaned in his arms, lifeless. After several years, he was enjoying being the first one to get Baba's attention after he came home. For hours Baba just sat there, soaking Peanut with his tears.

Peanut had kept his promise. The promise to save his friend at any cost, to be at his side till the last breath. And he did that, at the cost of his life. Several years had passed since then but his memories are still alive in our hearts.

I did not know that my life had a strange connection with the song. Never realised that I will also be left alone like the young girl in the song, longing for the love of my beloved friend.

Still feeling his warm presence, I can see him waiting for me to complete my homework. The memories of Ma feeding him like her own kid and Baba cajoling him after coming from the office still haunt me. Today I am listening to the song again. My eyes are closed and I am cherishing every moment we spent together. A thousand memories hit me while the song played, leaving my face wet with tears rolling down my cheeks. I open my eyes to look at him but the chair in front of me is empty. The record is moving over the spool creating a rattling sound as the song has finished but the words echo in my mind:

Kuchkuche Kalo She Jaate Spaniel

Tultule Ga Jeno Reshami Rumal

Ami Take Pushipol Namei Daktam

Pushipol E Shohore Chilo Ektai

Pushipol Pushipol Tumi Je Amar

Pushipol Pushipol Amio Tomar

Dujone Te Ekshathe Roj Bedatam

Pushipol E Shohore Chilo Ektai

He was so pitch-black Spaniel breed dog

His coat was like silk handkerchief

I called him by the name Pushipol

There was only one Pushipol in this town

Pushipol Pushipol you are mine

Pushipol Pushipol I am also yours

The duo were both on the move

Playing on the streets

There was only one Pushipol in this town

Story 3: The Thirst

"No, I won't cut the cake," Roma stomped her foot on the floor. "Call Mom. Where's she? MOM… MOM…," she cried and glanced around the hall to look for her mother.

The huge two-tier birthday cake lying on the table with seven beautiful candles seemed to mock her with the lines written on it:

"Happy Birthday Dearest Roma

from

Mom"

Sandhya, her nanny, took her in her arms and tried to calm her down. "Don't cry sweetie. Mamma had a very important party meeting today due to which she could not attend your birthday party. But see, she has got everything arranged for you!"

"No, I want her here right now! I won't cut the cake without her."

"*Beta*, today the tickets for the upcoming elections will be distributed and there are chances for her to get one. Try to understand and be a good girl."

"I don't understand why she always does this to me… party, meeting, tickets, election. I only want my mom," Roma said and started crying out loud, yelling at the top of her voice. Sandhya looked at Roma's friends who had huddled around the table and were staring at the cake constantly.

Everyone was waiting for the cake to be cut so that they could get their share of the oh-so-yummy-looking dessert.

"*Beta*, see everyone is waiting for you to cut the cake," Sandhya tried for one more time and wiped Roma's tears with a tissue. "Okay, I'll ask your mom to be with you on your next birthday. It's a deal. Promise!" she said, though deep inside her heart she knew it very well that Roma's mother lacked the natural instinct of motherhood. She was an over-ambitious lady who was least interested in her daughter's life.

"But every year she does the same thing," Roma protested.

"She keeps very busy *beta*. Now don't keep your friends waiting. Here, take this and cut the cake," Sandhya said and handed over the knife to Roma, while her voice choked with emotion and sympathy for the poor little girl. Roma took the knife with a heavy heart and cut the cake like a ritual but her mind was fixed on her mother.

"Everyone's parents are with them on their birthdays," she thought. "Okay, I understand papa cannot come. Sandhya aunty says no one can come from God's place. But mamma? She has not gone to God's home. Then why doesn't she come with me?" The questions kept bothering little Roma.

All the other children were enjoying the games and the food from the expensive restaurant, but Roma, the birthday girl, was sitting in a corner and fretting over her mother's attitude towards her.

The party was over and had left Roma with a feeling of dejection. At night, she was trying to sleep but couldn't close her eyes even for a moment as the feeling of humiliation, rejection and that she was unwanted filled her with bitterness. Her mother had not returned from her meeting yet and Roma had gone to sleep without meeting her even once the entire day. The pillow was soaked with tears that had flown from her eyes but now the tears had stopped and had left thin dry marks all over her cheeks. She was lying on her bed, hugging the huge pink teddy her mother had gifted for her birthday. A beautiful diamond locket in a gold chain was hanging from the neck of the teddy. This was also a gift from her mother that had arrived along with the teddy right in the middle of the party through a courier boy. Her friends had gone green with envy after seeing the gifts. But the person who received the expensive gifts was longing for something else altogether.

Sleep ditched Roma and her soul refused to rest with the hollowness that was growing inside her with every passing moment. After a while she heard the sound of a car stopping at their portico. Roma kissed the locket and clinched her eyes close, pretending to sleep with her arms around her teddy, when she heard footsteps nearing the door of her room. Her heartbeats started racing and she waited for her mother to come to her, trying to control her breath. Moments passed. One minute, two, three, four, five…but no one came inside. The footsteps passed her room and stopped at her mother's bedroom.

Roma was shocked. She was so sure her mother would come to the room to give her a tight hug with a goodnight kiss. Annoyed and irritated, she got up on her bed and threw the teddy with full force towards the mirror that was hanging on the wall. *Crack!* The locket hit the mirror and broke it into two pieces. Only a small portion in the middle held both the pieces together. That day something broke inside Roma too.

Fifteen years have passed after the incident. It is said that 'time heals all wounds.' Well, Roma's wounds were too deep to be healed. But yes, in due course of time, she had learned to bury them deep inside her heart where they were no longer visible. But from this pain, a matured political journalist was born who was famous for thrashing corrupt politicians with the might of her pen. This young, fierce journalist did not think twice to unmask even the most dangerous politicians who had criminal backgrounds.

"I have got a fantastic lead for you ma'am," her stringer, Pankaj's voice was brimming with excitement at the other end of the phone.

"Shoot!" Roma said, balancing the phone with her shoulder while she studied the papers of a story she was working upon.

"It's very confidential, about a very top shot politician," Pankaj said in a low tone. "Can we meet and discuss?"

"Okay, thirty minutes, Sitaram's *Dhaba*," Roma said and disconnected the phone.

After half an hour both of them were sitting in Sitaram's *Dhaba* discussing the involvement of a famous politician in a scam. A plate full of bread *pakoras* and tea in two tiny glass tumblers were on the table in front of them.

"Ma'am, this lady is very shrewd and cunning. She has been involved in numerous scams and murders, but no one could touch her in the past due to her connections with the criminals," Pankaj said while taking a bite of a bread *pakora*. After taking a sip of tea, he continued, "This is her newest scam where she has misappropriated an amount of 500 crore rupees. If you say, I will further investigate in the matter. A friend of mine will help us in collecting the evidence against her." He sighed and said again, "I don't know what she will do with all this money? I have done a basic research about her past and found that she has only one daughter. And this daughter of hers has no connection with her since the day she joined a boarding school. Her husband had also died long ago."

Roma smiled a meaningful smile. Her stringer was telling the background of her mother without realising that Roma also plays an important role in the story. "Who is she?" she was well aware of the name but still asked and almost instantly her mind went back to her teenage days.

Throughout her childhood years, she had yearned for her mother's love. It was the annual function at her school when she was in seventh standard. Roma was to play the lead role in a play that was to be performed during the function. Her mother was the chief guest of the function and Roma was riding on cloud nine with the thought that today her mother will definitely be present to watch the show.

In the evening, the function started with a welcome note and felicitation for the chief guest followed by a speech by her mother. She had clapped the hardest when her mother finished speaking. Her mother was seated right in the front row and Roma occasionally peeped from behind the curtains to ensure her presence. Eagerly waiting to perform in front of her mother, when Roma saw her mom leaving after the first performance, all her enthusiasm drained out of her. She wanted to shout, yell and cry but instead sat backstage, dumb and mute.

Her life is full of such instances. She never had the chance of being with her mother at home but these occasional functions and special days also passed without her mother's presence. In fact it is doubtful if her mother knows about her likes and dislikes that her nanny, Sandhya, is well aware of. A series of such incidents in her life gradually drew her away from her mother. They stayed in the same house like two strangers who hardly ever met each other. Everything that money could buy was overflowing in her life but the things whose value cannot be decided in tangible ways remained unachievable for her.

The innocent, adorable Roma had become a rebellious brat. With an extraordinarily sharp mind, she excelled in everything she did but she was continuously smouldering inside. Only the showers of her mother's love could soothe and relieve her from the agonising pain she had been suffering throughout her life. Her life was wandering like a leaf off the tree when the boarding school gave the raw energy in her mind a new direction and her thoughts were diverted towards a fruitful goal.

"It's the CM," Pankaj said in a very low volume. His voice appeared to be coming from a distance to Roma who was still wandering in her past. She was sitting there still, with her eyes glued to the bench.

"Ma'am, are you okay?" Pankaj asked worriedly on not getting any response from Roma.

"Hm? Hmm…Yeah," she said. "Okay, we are doing this story. Ask your friend to meet me here tomorrow, 5 pm sharp." Roma collected the shattered pieces from her past and got up, brushing her jeans with her hands.

Roma was not at all surprised by the revelation of the name of the politician involved in the scam. She has been witnessing several suspicious faces in her house since the day she grew up. During her stay in the boarding school of another state also she had heard many stories about her mother being involved in such scams. Her mother never came to meet her in her boarding and she also did not reveal her identity, so no one except the management staff was aware of her real identity. This helped her to mingle well with other students who unhesitatingly discussed about these matters in front of her.

Later, after doing her masters in journalism and joining a news channel, she had shifted to a PG, wanting to make her absence felt. But poor Roma did not know that she was meant to be forgotten and by shifting to a PG, she had made her mother's job much easier. For the past few years, she has been living with a new identity where everyone recognises Roma as a promising young journalist who had lost her parents in an accident long back.

Since then she has unveiled the faces of many corrupt politicians but this one was a real challenge for her. The story proved to be the toughest trial for Roma as with every piece of information, a new chapter of her mother's life got exposed in front of her. The more she learned about her, the more she detested her mother. But one thing that Roma failed to curb among all this chaos was her craving for the love of her mother that kept haunting her. In the middle of her sleep, she still longed to feel a soft hand caressing her hair with love. She tried hard but failed to crush her deepest desire–which was waiting for her mother to come and take Roma in her arms with affection.

The case was getting even more complicated with the discovery of new evidence. Its sensitivity could easily be gauged by the increasing number of threatening calls received by all who were involved in it. Roma had also received such calls but that did not stop her from doing her job. It was a Friday night and very few people were left in the office. Aiming to break the story before the upcoming election, she was putting all the loose ends together and arranging the evidences in chronological order and did not realise what the time was. When she completed everything and lifted her head from the laptop monitor to look at her watch, it was already past eleven in the night.

She stepped out of office. The still darkness of the night welcomed her with a deadly silence. There was no one to be seen on the long dark road. Roma glanced at the empty road and took the small lane leading to the metro station when suddenly she felt someone's presence behind her. She tried to turn but before that something cold and solid touched her shoulders and a heavy voice fell in her ears, "Leave this case or be ready to join your father in heaven." A deep chill went through her spine at the thought of standing at a gunpoint. She tried to look back but before that the man pushed her on the ground and vanished into the dark lane. She sighed. Now her mother has stooped to such a level that she has sent a shooter to threaten her, she thought. But it was difficult for her to accept the fact that her mother wanted to kill her for a mere win in the election. However, the incident made her even more determined to uncover the truth and she shifted all her focus to the story.

Unable to stop Roma, who was progressing like a huge storm towards her dream of winning the election, her mother called her for tea. Roma got a bit late in reaching the office and when she got there, a small envelope kept on the desk welcomed her with the very familiar letters written on it – *For Roma.* Nothing in this world could make her forget the way her mother writes *'R'*–large, round and a bit tilted towards the right. Instantaneously she recognised her mother's handwriting and unable to wait for another moment she took out the small piece of paper from the envelope.

'Roma, can you come for a cup of tea with me today evening?'

She smiled, a letter from her mother after fifteen years that appeared more like a sermon than a letter. No salutation, no wishes, no love message. Just a few words scribbled on a piece of paper. But she will go. How could she ignore her mother's wish? The whole day she kept thinking about the meeting and it seemed to be the longest day of her life. As soon as the clock struck five, she picked up her bag.

"Are you Ms Roma, the journalist?" a maid asked while opening the door.

"Yes," she said, confused at the thought if her mother was waiting for her daughter or the journalist Roma.

"She is waiting for you in the lawn. This way please," the maid showed her the way and went inside. Suddenly a very familiar face with two affectionate eyes appeared in front of her.

"How are you *beta*? It's been so long since I saw you!" Sandhya said and held Roma's face in her palms. Roma stood there dumbstruck for a moment. She did not realise when her eyes got moist. Fine lines of age had started appearing on Sandhya's face and her pitch-black hair had turned salt and pepper now. One thing that remained unchanged was the love and affection in her eyes for Roma.

"I am perfectly fine. I didn't know you were still working here," she said, choked with emotion.

"*Beta*, your mother has ill intentions for you. Be cautious and do not eat or drink anything. They are poisoned!" she whispered in a frightened tone and vanished behind the curtains. Roma felt as if someone had made her sniff chloroform and the nerves in her head had turned numb. Though her well-wishers had warned her about the intentions of her mother, the daughter inside her had refused to believe them.

Somehow collecting her senses, Roma went to the lawn where her mother was sitting on a garden sofa, cross-legged. "Come Roma," her mother said and put the file she was reading on the center table. Draped in an off-white Sanganeri cotton sari, her mother was looking graceful. Roma slowly reached the nearest chair and sat without saying a word.

"How are you?" she asked Roma but her voice was as cold as her face. Roma kept on staring at her face unable to believe that her mother had not changed a bit in the last fifteen years. Roma had expected an entirely different kind of meeting. She had been daydreaming the entire day about this meeting–when her mother would come running to her and take her into her arms. But nothing was happening like she had imagined.

She smiled feebly as words failed this noted journalist who had always been the mistress of words. "I heard you are working as a journalist in a news channel," her mother said arriving straight to the point. Something started boiling inside Roma and she felt the same agonising pain that had been a regular companion throughout her childhood.

"Yes," Roma replied in a low voice.

"Good. I have heard a lot about your work and want you to excel in your life," her mother said and took out a white envelope from the file that was kept on the table. "Here, take this," she said.

"What is this?" Roma asked, surprised.

"This is your appointment letter as an editor in a well-known channel. You have to report within two days."

Roma looked at the envelope that held the keys that could open the doors to her dream job and then said with a smile, "... and joining this job means I will have to forget about all the stories that I am currently working upon."

"Of course," her mother replied immediately.

"No thanks, Mom. I cannot accept this," Roma said and got up to leave.

"Okay, it's your wish..." her mother's face became stern, "... but let's have a cup of tea together for which I have called you."

Roma put her bag on the center table and sat down again in front of her mother without uttering a word. Her mother called for the maid who brought a tray with two cups and a teapot. Her mother prepared a cup and gave it to Roma. Suddenly Sandhya's frightened face flashed in front of her eyes and she gave a meaningful look to the steaming hot tea swirling in the cup.

"It's impossible," said a daughter's love for mother.

"It's risky," said experience.

"It's pointless," said reason.

"Go for it!" whispered her heart.

She lifted the cup and emptied it in one go. After all, this was the first time her mother had taken the pain to do *something* for her.

Story 4: Selective Secularism

My Grandmother is a really secular person. She never differentiates between a Hindu, a Muslim and a Kristan (as she calls a Christian). The only religion that she practises with most vehemence is Brahmanism. Every person who is not a Brahmin is forbidden in her territory. As far as my memory goes back, I have seen her keeping a fair amount of distance with every person who is not a Brahmin.

"Sorry, I don't take anything prepared by a Kayasth, not even a glass of water from their hands," she had said bluntly to Ghosh aunty once when she offered my grandma a *rasagulla,* which was Ghosh aunty's first lesson at her cookery class of Bengali sweets.

Ghosh aunty's face became red and then turned grey as if someone had rubbed a handful of soot on it. I looked at my parents from the corner of my eyes. Both of them were staring at the floor as if waiting for goddess Sita to come and take them with her.

But that day the whole episode had ended with a great event. To make up for the comments made by my grandma, we all took a second helping of the delicious sweet, singing mile-long phrases of praise for Ghosh aunty. Anyway, the sweet was worth it.

Thamma, as I call my grandma, is also very particular about the rituals and duties that the Indian society of her times wants a widow to perform. Draped in a crisp white cotton sari with '*chandan ka tika*' adorning her forehead, she was always reciting the names of Hindu Gods and goddesses.

Being a God-fearing person, she always wanted to be in their good books.

Well, if you conclude from the above description of my dear Thamma that she is an illiterate, nagging lady like many old Hindu widows of the late 20th century, then you are highly mistaken. She is an educated lady who loved to be abreast with the latest happenings via newspapers and a darling who envelops all of us with the cosy warmth of her love and care. And did I mention that she used to go on dates with my grandpa to watch English movies? No? Oops! So let me enlighten you with the fact that she enjoyed going to Regal, Rivoli, Plaza and Odeon with my grandpa to watch classic English movies. If you are scratching your head trying to digest the paradox then allow me to help you understand the situation. My grandpa loved to watch English classics with Thamma and took her to watch them together. Now that's another story where he had to work hard in making her qualified enough to understand the language by teaching her English.

So now I believe you have a fairly good idea of my Thamma's mind-blowing personality that is an amalgamation of the old and the new. A mix of the pre-independent and post-independent modern India.

Okay, coming back to the point where I was telling you about her viewpoint on secularism. She was happily living with her preconceived notions on religion, when we all got the shock of our life. That dreadful day gave us all a chill through our spine when we saw Thamma suddenly falling off her chair while she was reading the Bengali newspaper. We all rushed to hold her, but by the time we could reach her, she was already leaning on the handle of the chair. Baba and Ma rushed her to the hospital where she was admitted for a thorough check-up.

Thamma had paid a hefty price for her God-fearing rituals and frequent fasts. Suffering from acute anaemia, she needed an immediate blood transfusion to revive and come back to consciousness. Baba rushed to the blood bank to arrange blood for her. When he didn't come back even after a good half an hour, I came out of the room where Thamma was admitted to look for him. What I saw in the passage outside the room was enough to confuse me. Baba was moving all along the passage, panicking and rubbing his hands together in anguish. This was a shock for me, as I had never seen him like this before. Baba is a very composed person and this kind of behaviour was completely unlike him.

"What's the matter Baba?" I asked, trying to calm him down. "Why are you so nervous?"

"Her blood group is O negative, and the only unit available at the moment in the blood bank is of Abdul's," he said. Baba's words were shaking and small droplets of sweat had covered his forehead even in the air-conditioned atmosphere of the hospital.

"So how does it matter? And how come you know the name of the donor?" I asked impatiently.

"I had enquired from the blood bank, it's Abdul, a Muslim," he said, words barely coming out of his mouth.

"How could you say like this Baba?" I couldn't believe my ears as Baba said this. "He is also a human like all of us and his blood matches with Thamma. That's all we should care about."

"I know, but you know Ma very well. When she regains consciousness, the first question she will ask is the donor's name. And God only knows what will happen next," he said.

The matter was serious and needed Ma's intervention. I knew only she could handle the situation and convince Baba to take the right decision. I ran to her who was sitting beside Thamma's bed in the ward and asked her to convince Baba. After about an hour, her persuasion and Abdul's blood triumphed in bringing Thamma back to consciousness.

Thamma had never expected to land in such a situation due to her everlasting fasts that she observed every second day to please her Gods. The whole incident had shaken her so much that she immersed many of her rituals and 'fasts' in river Ganges while coming back from the hospital.

Next day we all were chatting over a cup of tea in the evening. Thamma was also participating and contributing her bit every now and then. With a bowl of hot spinach soup in her hands, she was having a spoonful at regular intervals. We were all teasing her for the incident when suddenly she asked me, "Who gave me the blood?"

Almost instantly there was pin-drop silence in the room. Baba, who was going to say something, immediately pulled back his unspoken words and laughter inside his mouth and started searching the newspaper. Ma suddenly remembered that her 'imaginary' *dal* was burning on the stove and went inside the kitchen to revive it. I slowly got up and walked towards Thamma. Holding her from the shoulders, I looked straight into her eyes and said

"Abdul, his name is Abdul, Thamma."

She looked at me for a moment, sipped another spoonful of the soup and said, "May God bless him. He has done a very pious job."

Story 5: Bribe

It was an October evening. Winter was slowly sneaking its way into the atmosphere and making its presence felt with the slight chill in the air. It was already dark outside when I stepped out of the office. Vehicles were moving along on the busy streets, making it very difficult for pedestrians like me to walk on them. As it is in a town like Lucknow, everyone has very graciously accepted the narrow lanes meant for the walkers as an extension of the main road, leaving almost negligible space for them. The streets basked in neon glory from the streetlights above me while I made my way through them.

The day had been very hectic. Preparing for the meeting to be held the next day was a tedious job and my mind was still filled with all the files and the presentations to be made. Being a personal assistant to the director of the organisation demanded a lot from me. However, now I wanted to be home and be with my little darling Mini. Four years had passed but it seemed like yesterday when little Mini had become a part of my and Prabha's lives. When I saw her for the first time in the hospital, she was sleeping in a cradle and reminded me of a tiny porcelain doll, stark white with flushes of pink around her cheeks. I have always felt babies are beautiful, drooling, adorable tiny creatures that make everyone's life beautiful. Their radiance spreading happiness wherever they go. But this one was special; I had developed an unknown connection with her the moment I saw her. When I took my little angel in my arms for the first time, I was so astonished and thrilled that the moment is still fresh in my memory.

She comes running to me every day and greets me with her sweet smile in the evening when I return home, and jumps into my lap, putting her tiny arms around my neck. Mini is a chatterbox and my exhaustions are washed away by her innocent talks. To see Mini quiet is unnatural and I could not bear it long. I have always liked her chirpy and cheerful.

Engrossed in Mini's thoughts, I was striding towards my home, which was not very far from my office. When I entered the lane near my house, I was welcomed by the strong aroma of spicy hot samosas that were being made in the local sweet shop. This shop happened to be situated in the next lane to my house and was famous for its delicious sweets and savouries.

The smell of the samosas enticed me and all of a sudden I felt a rumbling in my stomach. I got some packed with me to enjoy with a cup of hot tea. "Mini will also be very glad to see the samosas, her favourite," I thought and a smile flashed on my lips. Thinking about Mini and the samosas, I turned towards my house and pressed the doorbell.

My thoughts of playing with Mini over a cup of tea and snacks got crushed when Prabha opened the door. "Oh! So you are home finally. I was trying to call you for a while now, but there was no network on your phone," she said, wiping small beads of sweat from her forehead with the corner of her *dupatta*. "What happened? Is everything fine? You look tensed!" I asked, worried at the sight of thin lines of tension around her forehead and eyes.

"Mini is not well. She was perfectly fine till noon but towards the evening, she became feverish. I just checked the temperature and it has risen to 102 degrees Fahrenheit."

I felt the whole world revolving in front of me and my heart started beating so fast that I could hear it. The thought of Mini running such a high temperature sent a shiver down my spine. Mini becomes very irritable whenever she falls sick and I always like to see her fresh and smiling face.

"Did you see the doctor?" I asked.

"How could I take her alone? She is almost unconscious," Prabha replied.

"Okay, I am bringing the doctor home," I said and started out to get the doctor. Usually we went to the local doctor who had his clinic in our colony. There were barely two to three patients in the clinic and I sat on a chair kept in the corner, waiting for them to go. When the doctor was free, I asked him to visit our house and check Mini.

Mini was still unconscious and her face looked pale when the doctor came. Prabha was standing at the bedside staring lovingly at Mini's face as the doctor checked her. To control the fever, he took out an injection from his bag and Prabha closed her eyes tightly as the needle pierced Mini's arm. The love of a mother feared that the needle would tear her darling daughter into pieces.

"Don't worry. She will be fine by morning," said the doctor, handing me some tablets to give Mini after dinner and turned towards Prabha saying, "Give her some light food when she wakes up."

I was desperately longing for a cup of tea and looked at Prabha when the doctor left, with a hope of getting some to relax my temporal nerves. But my hopes were flattened when I found her sitting beside Mini, rolling her hands over Mini's head. Prabha's face looked pale with fatigue and stress and not wanting to disturb her, I brushed aside the thought of getting tea and headed towards the washroom to change and freshen up.

After showering, I felt better but the cramps in my stomach time and again reminded me that it had been more than six hours since I had had my lunch. I was in dire need of some fresh fuel to keep me going. When I entered the room again rubbing my face with the towel, I found Prabha still sitting beside Mini's bed, pressing down the ice bag on her forehead.

"Please sit here and press this ice bag on her head," Prabha said when she saw me entering the room and got up to go to the kitchen saying, "Meanwhile I will quickly prepare the meal."

The absence of the regular caffeine dose in my blood had given me a mild headache that was annoying me way too much to even think about doing anything right now. I simply wanted to have the dinner and sleep at the moment. I opened my mouth to utter a few words in protest but by the time I could find the right words, Prabha was already gone leaving me with no choice. I quietly picked the ice bag and sat beside Mini on the bed.

Fever had snatched all the glow from her face and Mini was looking very pale in her sleep. I gently touched her forehead to check the severity of fever and took a sigh of relief to find it diminishing. "Mamma...," Mini murmured in her sleep, which suddenly made me feel jealous of Prabha. Mini was calling for her mamma even in her sleep. I wanted her to get up and play with me like she did every other day. I do not know how much time passed beholding her innocent face when I got startled by Prabha's footsteps. When I looked up, I found Prabha standing beside me with a cup of tea and some biscuits. Placing the cup on the side table she said, "You must be tired. Have some tea."

I was delighted to see the cup with steaming hot tea and felt as if the tension along the side of my temporal nerves was releasing. "Prabha never forgets about my requirements even if she is busy with other tasks." I smiled and picked up the cup. After about an hour, Prabha came again to call me for dinner. She bent to touch Mini's forehead and the nerves of her forehead got relaxed when she saw that the fever had subsided.

"You have the dinner and after that you may sit with Mini while I eat. Till then I will feed her this *khichdi,*" Prabha said sitting beside Mini with the bowl of *khichdi* that she had prepared for her.

I went to the dining room and eagerly removed the lid of the bowl. The potato pieces floating in the yellow curry appeared to mock me. I wrinkled my nose and opened the lid of the hot case. There were *chapattis* in it. My hunger evaporated with the sight of the food and with it, my will to eat the food.

"You know I don't like potato curry. At least you could have made some *parathas,*" I called out.

"You know I didn't get much time with Mini being so unwell. This is what I could prepare in such short time," she said apologetically.

Dejected, I pulled out the chair making a loud noise against the floor to convey my disapproval of the food prepared by her, and sat down to eat. With a lot of effort I gulped down two *chapattis* with potato curry and got up. On returning to the room I found Prabha still feeding Mini very patiently. She was carefully placing small portions of *khichdi* from the bowl in Mini's mouth. At the same time she kept on wiping the extra portion off her face with a napkin. Relieved to see Mini better now, I went near her, caressed her head and said with a smile, "My baby looks fine now. She will be completely alright by tomorrow."

Mini smiled meekly at me and continued eating. Suddenly she vomited everything on the floor and herself. Disgusted with the view, I immediately went to the other room. After a good fifteen minutes when I entered the room again, Prabha had already cleaned the floor and changed Mini's clothes.

"Give her the tablet that the doctor has given," Prabha said to me, but by this time I had already spread my legs on the long chair and opened the newspaper that I had left half-read in the morning. I was in no mood to get up now and wanted some moments of respite.

"I am damn tired and can't get up now," I said in an irritated tone while staring at the newspaper.

Prabha stood there quietly for a moment looking at me and went inside to bring the medicine. I don't know how she managed alone but by the time she finished dinner and was done with the cleaning, the clock had struck 11:30 pm.

"Mini will sleep in our room today," Prabha said taking Mini in her lap to shift to the room. Already aware of the outcome of any discussion with her, I preferred not to say anything and followed her quietly.

"No! Don't switch the fan on," she said quickly as she saw me approaching the switchboard to switch the fan on.

"But I can't sleep without the fan!" I protested.

"Okay, then you may go to the other room and sleep," she said firmly patting Mini's forehead softly to make her sleep.

Irritated, I went to the other room to sleep. In the middle of the night, I suddenly felt my throat drying and got up to drink some water. When I peeped inside the other room to check Mini, I found Prabha sitting quietly on the bed with Mini's head in her lap, driving the mosquitoes away from her with one of her hands and patting her forehead with the other. The sight filled me with a feeling that was a blend of surprise and admiration. How could Prabha manage so much? Attending to anyone sick is beyond my capacity, especially Mini when she becomes very irritable and no longer remains the usual self. I like a chirpy and happy Mini giggling and playing with me.

Next day I got up with the sound of utensils coming from the kitchen. I looked at the wall clock and again went to sleep as it was a Sunday and I was in no hurry. After about fifteen minutes Prabha came to the room with a cup of tea and woke me up.

"Can you please sit with Mini for a while till I prepare the breakfast?" she said handing the tea to me.

"How is she now?" I asked.

"Much better. There is no fever now."

I got up with the cup and went to the other room where Mini was playing joyfully on the bed with the soft toys. She smiled and jumped over me with joy when she saw me. Relieved to see her chirpy and playful again, I joined her in the play.

Suddenly she cried, "Mamma, I am thirsty." Instantly I remembered the previous day's incident when Mini was calling Prabha in her sleep. Something pinched inside me. Why didn't Mini ask water from me?

A sudden insecurity filled my heart and I asked her, "Mini, whom do you love more? Mamma or papa?"

Prabha, who had come to the room with the glass of milk, stood there with a smile on her face to listen what she had to say. Her eyes, full of curiosity, were glued on Mini. But Mini found this question very tricky. How could she say whom she loved more? Unable to decide what to say, she kept on looking at our faces.

I asked again "Tell me *beta*? I will bring your favourite toy and a big box of chocolates for you."

"Really?" Mini's eyes twinkled at the thought of getting gifts and chocolates.

"Yes!"

"I love you more," she said instantly and hugged me tightly.

Prabha's smile vanished. But she quickly recovered and brushed it off as if nothing happened. She wiped her eyes and went and kissed Mini on her forehead and gave her the glass of milk. I looked at her in awe. I felt a wave of guilt hit me. How could I be so selfish? How could I take away the love and gratitude that Prabha deserved? As I contemplated my actions, Prabha handed me another cup of tea and smiled at me warmly. Before I could say anything she walked away to the kitchen. I looked at Mini; a milk moustache adorned her face as she giggled at me. I knew I had to set things right.

"Mini, Papa can buy you a million gifts but none of them would be as special as the gift of the kind of unconditional love your mother showers on us every day. She selflessly toils every day just to bring a smile to our face. You're the luckiest daughter in the world… and I'm the luckiest husband," I whispered, hugging her tightly against my chest.

Story 6: Forever

The security check was over and there was still an hour left for the flight to take off. I headed towards a sofa kept at the corner of the waiting lounge when I saw the bookstore that happened to be located in front of it. With the intention of passing some time, I was about to step into the store when an irritated female voice fell in my ears, "This is simply ridiculous. Now I will have to read the translated works of Gulzar Sahab?" I looked in the direction from where the voice had come and found a lady holding a book, arguing with the salesman for not keeping original works of Gulzar Sahab in the store. Her back was towards me and I could not see her face. But one thing that I could make out very well about her from the conversation was that she was a great admirer of Gulzar Sahab. This took me back to my college days and almost instantly another face flashed in front of my eyes. Swati, my childhood friend, was also an ardent fan of the great writer and used to go mad when anyone showed her the translated version of his works.

"You know Supriya," she used to say "every word written by him is an ocean of expressions, and these people think they can hold the same depth in the translated copies." She was crazy over his works and had sent him a novel also requesting to make a film over it. A light laugh came out of my mouth with the thought and that drew the attention of the salesman who hurriedly came towards me to get rid of the lady. She quickly turned to say something and our eyes met. For a moment, everything appeared to become still around me and then both of us jumped with surprise.

It was none other than Swati who was standing in front of me after twenty four long years. I looked at her from head to toe. She had not changed a bit and was looking the same as she did two decades ago. Only her long, thick, black hair that used to be tied in a braid was left free now but that had added an additional charm to her beauty. Her peach and milk complexion was glowing with an extra radiance in a light pink *salwar-kameez* and her kohl-stained large deep brown eyes appeared to be holding a thousand mysteries behind their cheerful expression like they did earlier. It was very difficult to say by looking at her that she was in her late forties. Overwhelmed to see the best friend of my teenage days in front of me, words refused to come out of my mouth and I simply stepped ahead to give her a tight, warm hug.

"I can't believe my eyes!" she exclaimed. "I never thought I'd be meeting you again. This is so wonderful!" Brimming with happiness, she couldn't decide what to do and finally unable to figure out how to react at the situation, she dragged me to the nearest sofa. I silently followed her but my mind was exploding with a million thoughts. Every day that we had spent together and everything that happened during those years of my life rolled in front of my eyes like an old movie. But amidst all this joy of reunion, I was still trying to decide if I owned the full credit of her excitement or there was something else that was the cause of her happiness. One more thing was constantly troubling me and I feared how she would react after learning about where I was going.

"When did you come to India?" finally I managed to ask her.

"Just now. And guess where am I going from here?" she was overflowing with excitement.

"Where?" I asked and my heart skipped a beat fearing what she would say next.

"Lucknow, to attend Rahul's wedding," she said and my heart sank. This was perhaps exactly what I feared to hear from her.

"Oh."

"What do you mean by 'oh'?" Swati said and got carried away again. "Don't you remember Rahul? My cousin sister's son who used to follow us everywhere that we went and we had to bribe him with a bar of chocolate to make him stay at home."

Yes, I remembered Rahul very well. He was Anuradha didi's son who used to visit Swati's house every year during summer vacations. Anuradha didi was very close to Swati's parents and made it a point to visit them every year. Rahul was born in front of us when we were in school and held a special bond with both of us. When he grew up a little, he started following us everywhere making it very difficult for us to go anywhere. Ultimately we had to bribe him with chocolates and *Gems*, his favourite, to get some time for ourselves. That Rahul has turned into a handsome grown up young man now who is working in a reputed IT firm and getting married next week.

"How are Uncle and Aunty?" I asked Swati. For a moment the gleam in her eyes was covered by a sad look, but she quickly brushed it off and said in a low tone, "They are no more."

"When?" I asked in dismay.

"Ten years ago, in an accident. Both of them left, leaving me all alone in this world," she sighed.

A feeling of sadness mixed with empathy for Swati enveloped me and I asked, "Alone?"

"Yes, I didn't marry," she said, and instantly a name rang in my mind…Shekhar. After a silence of few moments, she again restored herself and said, "I am so excited to meet everyone after so many years. You know, I lost touch with everyone after the death of mamma and pa, but when I got the card for Rahul's marriage, I immediately decided to come to India."

Perhaps she did not expect this and I also could not tell her that like her, I was also going to Lucknow to attend the same wedding. She was constantly talking but I was mute, wandering in the past, worried what to say if she asks about Shekhar.

Swati and me were doing our engineering in Electronics and Communication and were in B.Tech second year when we badly felt the need of someone who could give us some tips on C++ and Java. Shekhar, who lived in the same society, incidentally happened to be in the same college as we did. He was our senior and we had a casual acquaintance with him. After learning about his being a student of computer science, both of us did a dance of joy. Unable to decide among ourselves about who was going to ask him for help, both of us went to him to ask for the help one day. He was getting out of the college gate to return home when we caught hold of him. He gladly accepted the responsibility and our tuition started from the next day. Initially he taught us in the college library, but later he began taking the classes in his house where he was staying with his elder brother.

The tuition lessons were over in a couple of weeks but all three of us were tied in a bond of friendship. All three of us enjoyed spending time and going out together. Everything was fine for the initial few months but after some time I started noticing Swati's face shining with a special glow and she could not lift her eyes in shyness at the mention of

Shekhar's name. "Hey! What has happened to you?" I teased her one day. "I hope you are not in love with Shekhar?" She blushed and nodded slowly and I jumped on my seat with excitement.

"When did this happen? I have always been with you whenever you met him," I asked again finding it difficult to absorb the news. "And Shekhar? What about him? He knows?" unable to hold my excitement, I was piercing her with a million questions and she was sitting there smiling, quietly staring the floor.

Not getting any response from her, I pushed her slightly with my finger, "Hey, tell me everything."

"Actually he gave me a letter the other day confessing about his love for me in it," she said fumbling.

"When?"

"When I was going to buy my practical note book."

And thus started their journey of love for which I was the witness at every step. Now all three of us made a gang and spent most of our free time together. Not to let her parents know about the love blooming within her for Shekhar, I was always dragged with them wherever they went. I still remember it was Shekhar's birthday and Swati wanted to spend some time alone with him. And it was me who had to pay the price of being a good friend to them. Both of them were having a gala time celebrating Shekhar's birthday and I was getting soaked in the evening dew while sitting in a park with a book, so that her parent's wouldn't get to know about it.

It was our last year of engineering and we all were busy planning our career paths. I had decided to join a job whereas Swati was planning to go for her MS in the US. She was preparing her applications for various universities when I directly asked her one day, "Have you discussed about this with Shekhar?"

She did not say anything and silently kept on filling the form. "Do you hear me? I am talking to YOU, Swati!" I shook her hands, agitated. My frustration had seeped into my voice as well and I shouted at her when I did not get any response from the other end.

"Yes," came the brief reply.

"And what have you both decided about this?"

"We have broken up. I need to go for my further studies and he can't leave the country," she said.

"But why?" I asked, unable to make sense of whatever she was saying.

"I want to settle in the US and do not want to come back. Shekhar says he has to stay back here in India with his parents. His brother has already shifted abroad and now he cannot leave his parents alone."

I felt the world turned upside down and tried to take one last chance.

"Then why don't you come back after your studies are over?" I asked.

"No, I have dreamt of settling in the US since my childhood and cannot compromise with my dreams for anything," she said coldly.

I was trying hard to get over the news. The fact that she will be going forever leaving Shekhar behind was making me feel miserable. I had seen their love bloom and wanted it to reach to a conclusion.

Finally the day arrived when Swati was leaving for America. With tears filled in her eyes, she hugged me to say goodbye and stole a glance at Shekhar who was standing in one corner. After promising to send us her new address soon, she sat in the car with wet eyes and waved goodbye for the last time.

Initially, we wrote to each other every week but gradually the frequency between the letters started growing from a week to fifteen days, one month and eventually, with time and our involvement in other matters, exchange of letters ceased between us. The last I had heard about her from her parents was that she was pursuing her PhD. But when her parents also joined her after uncle's retirement, this thin link between us also broke.

Shekhar was initially devastated by the decision taken by Swati but later we all were successful in pulling him out of the situation. He was adamant about not getting married and several persuasions by friends did not help but after few years he surrendered before the wish of his parents and got married. My connection with Swati was lost but I was in regular touch with Shekhar as he had shifted with his wife in the house in our society where he lived with his brother earlier.

With time, I also got married and shifted to Delhi with my husband but did not lose touch with him. Whenever I went to my parent's house, I made it a point to meet him. Swati's name was never mentioned between us, and gradually Shekhar's wife filled the void that was created in our friendship due to her absence.

"How is everyone in India? Do you happen to meet them?" Swati held my hands within her palms and asked again. Her voice brought me back to the present and I looked at her face trying to figure out whom she meant by *them*. If she was asking about Shekhar, then yes, I used to meet him often. But if she was asking about Anuradha didi, then I felt like screaming at top of my voice, "How could I? Did you ever bother to stay in touch or come along to meet us? Then how do you expect me to stay in touch with your cousin sister?"

I stole a glance at her left palm to look for something and whatever I found, hit me like an electric shock. She has not forgotten him yet. The silver ring with the fake diamonds still adorned her third finger, a total mismatch with the other expensive jewellery pieces that she wore. This silver ring had its own story. It was Swati's birthday and I was getting ready for the treat that she had promised to both of us, Shekhar and me. Suddenly the doorbell rang and when I opened it, I found Shekhar standing there. I looked at him with questioning eyes. He took out a small box from his pocket and handed it to me.

"What is this?" I asked. "A gift for Swati."

"Then give it to her, why you are giving this to me?" I asked in surprise while opening the box. A beautiful silver ring studded with American diamonds was sparkling inside the box.

"Today *you* present this to her on my behalf. I will give her a ring when I will be able to slide it in her finger in everyone's presence," and saying this, he hurriedly turned and stepped down the stairs.

I gave it to Swati but never missed a chance after that to tease them by narrating the incident. Swati had worn the ring in the third finger of her left hand saying emotionally, "I will only remove this when Shekhar will replace this with another ring in front of our parents." I had smiled then but today when I found the same ring in her finger after twenty four years, my heart was filled with sadness. Unaware of my thoughts, Swati was still wandering in the thoughts of the marriage she was going to attend.

"You know I got so busy in my research that never got any time to visit India. And like it happens with relatives, everyone went about their doing their own business after mamma and pa's death. I only received these occasional wedding and engagement cards," she sighed. "But when I got the card of Rahul's marriage, I immediately decided to come to India. I still can't believe that cute, little Rahul has grown up so much, he is getting married!" she said with a twinkle in her eyes. But will this twinkle last when she learns about Rahul's bride? I thought and a sinking feeling started growing within me.

Anuradha didi's in-laws lived in Lucknow, the native city of Shekhar. When she got acquainted with Shekhar at Swati's house, she and her family started visiting them in Lucknow as well. She liked the family and from the day Shekhar's daughter, Sudha, was born, she had visualized her as her future daughter-in-law and was waiting for the appropriate time to ask for her hand. When Sudha completed her graduation, Anuradha didi landed at her grandparent's house one fine day with a box of sweets and the marriage proposal. Shekhar and his family also agreed to the proposal and now Sudha and Rahul were getting married in Lucknow next week. I was attending the marriage from Shekhar's side.

"Do you know who the bride is?" I asked her slowly.

"No, I saw the card but didn't pay much attention to the bride's details. It was enough for me to learn that it is Rahul, Anuradha didi's son, who is getting married," she said. "And I also wanted to visit Lucknow once," she said and quickly removed her eyes from me, perhaps to escape from the very obvious questions that could follow.

So she has not forgotten him. She could not remove the gift from her fingers that Shekhar had given her so many years ago. And Lucknow? Why did she want to visit Lucknow? I did not ask her. I knew her heart was bleeding inside her and I did not want to scratch her wounds further.

"It is Sudha," I said looking straight into her eyes, "Shekhar's daughter. I am also going to attend the same marriage."

Her face immediately turned white as if someone had extracted every drop of blood from her. She tried to hold her breath for a couple of moments and then said, "How could Anuradha didi do this to me? She knew about Shekhar and me. At least she could have written two lines telling me about the bride. How could she be so sure that I will not attend this marriage either?" Swati said and large teardrops appeared at the corner of her eyes.

Words had ceased between us and we were sitting there, silent. After a good ten minutes, she asked me, "Can you do me a favour?"

"What?" I asked her in response to her question, feeling a lump in my throat. Swati slowly removed the ring from her finger and placed it on my palm saying, "Give this to Shekhar when you meet him."

"And what about you? You will not come with me?"

"No, I will stay here tonight in any hotel and fly back tomorrow," she said, wiping the tears with a tissue that were rolling down her cheeks.

I could not say anything, wondering if she was expecting Shekhar to remain unmarried throughout his life, too.

The boarding announcement was made for the flight to Lucknow. I got up from the sofa, holding the ring in my fist, somewhat nervous with the new responsibility imposed over me by Swati.

Everyone was enjoying the celebrations at the wedding but my excitement had all gone away with Swati. I could not be a part of the wedding for a moment. The entire time Swati's face, full of tears, rolled in front of my eyes. When all the rituals were over and everyone was blessing the bride and the groom, I slipped the ring in Sudha's finger because I did not have the courage to return it to Shekhar and at the same time could not break my promise also. By giving the ring to Shekhar's daughter I had brought it to where it belonged, in Shekhar's life. I looked from the corner of my eyes at Shekhar who froze seeing the ring. After the bride went with the groom's family, Shekhar called me in a room and asked, "She had come here?"

"Who?" I counter-questioned, pretending not to understand his question.

"Swati? Did she come here? Tell me. Did you meet her?" Shekhar asked impatiently holding both of my hands tight. I could not answer and kept on looking at him. Shekhar had also not forgotten her and still yearns for her. Today I realised that the dust can only cover your memories for some time but the feelings that lay buried beneath them remain the same, forever. It's just that you have to brush the dust aside to get hold of the same feelings again. His grip on my hands was increasing and the pain from his heart was getting transferred to my hands.

Story 7: The Wait

"*Bhabhi*, I need these holidays badly. Please *Bhabhi*," Gita, my maid, pleaded while cutting the vegetables.

I lifted my eyes from the laptop monitor and tried to read her eyes, but they were completely blank like an empty canvas.

"But last month also you had taken leave for one week," I said, recalling the marathon of tasks that I had to accomplish single-handedly in her absence. Being a working woman, that too a scientist, demands a lot of my time. The day passes in a jiffy at the office after which I am left with very little time for myself. These moments are very precious for me that I spend with my family. It's the perfect time for me to relax and enjoy the company of the people I love and care about the most. Without a domestic help, life becomes a mechanical routine that revolves around the office, kitchen and other household tasks. A sudden wave of anxiety hit me at the thought of managing everything for one month without Gita.

"Please *Bhabhi*, if I don't go now, I will lose my share in the farms and inherited property of my in-laws," she said again.

Gita had lost her husband twenty years ago in a road accident. Her in-laws had played an equally important role in her destiny to make her cursed life even more miserable. Being a self-respecting woman, she left her in-laws' place the moment she felt she was being exploited due to the new status after the death of her husband: 'widow.'

"Gita, you should have opened a *dhaba,*" her husband used to say every time he tasted the food prepared by her. "We could have earned a fortune with this talent of yours." Gita used to feel on the top of the world when she heard such words from her husband. But now when he was not around, the same talent had helped her earn her living respectfully in a city like Lucknow. For the past three years, she has been working as a cook in our house. With my never-ending meetings and conferences, I seldom got any time to cook and Gita had been the respite I was looking for.

Gita was a good cook and she had adapted well to the palettes of my kids and husband. The transition from preparing *mutton rogan josh* with an inch of oil floating at the top to healthy salads and low-oil curries was smooth and instantaneous. The thought itself of sending her on one month's leave sent shiver down my spine. But on the other hand, how could I deprive Gita of what was rightfully hers?

"Okay, you will have to give me a substitute for the period you are on leave," I said.

"Sure *Bhabhi*, I will send my neighbour Kamla. She is also looking for a job," she said, elated with the approval of her leave.

"And what if she doesn't leave after you are back?" I teased her with a mischievous smile. "Or I find her cooking better than yours?"

"No, she is looking for a job for a temporary period," she said and the matter ended there.

Next day Gita was standing at the door with a young girl, who was barely twenty-one years old and had a small kid in her arms.

"*Namaste Bhabhi*, this is Kamla about whom I had spoken to you yesterday," Gita said. Kamla greeted me with a shy smile.

I called them inside the hall and sat on the sofa. Kamla followed me quietly into the room and sat on the floor in front of me.

Draped in a bottle green sari with a bright golden border, Kamla was still looking like a new bride with her hands full of matching green and golden glass bangles, silver *pajeb* (anklets) and artificial golden jewellery. Her shiny black hair was well oiled and tied up neatly into a thick braid which was complimenting her dark skin. She was not beautiful but there was something about her that would make everyone take a second look at her.

"You are very young. Will you be able to manage everything?" I asked her.

"*Ji Memsahib*," she said.

"You may call me *Bhabhi*," I said. The words *Memsahib* had always made me feel uncomfortable. It made me feel like I had been transported to the colonial era and I was imitating a lady barking orders at the servile help.

"She is very smart *Bhabhi*. You will not have any complaints," Gita advocated about her.

"And what about your baby? How will you manage with such a small kid?" I pointed towards her baby who was hardly six months old.

"I will leave him with my neighbours. They have agreed to look after him while I am out for work."

"And your husband? What does he do?"

She looked up at me and hastily removed her glance. But in that fraction of a moment I had seen the small drops of tears at the corners of her large kohl-stained eyes.

"He is absconding *Bhabhi* since last year," Gita said. "He was working as a security guard in a company."

I could sense that there was something that was bothering Kamla. Her inner turmoil was evident in the hollowness that prevailed in her eyes. Not wanting to hurt her anymore, I asked her to come from the next day.

Kamla was an intelligent girl and she picked up everything very quickly. Initially her duty included only preparing the meals but eventually she started spending most of her time of the day in my kitchen. Though her serving us for long hours had made my life much simpler, I worried about her baby who had to spend the whole day without his mother.

"Kamla, how can you leave such a small baby with your neighbours for the whole day?" I asked her one day.

"I have left him with my parents. It was becoming difficult to handle him alone," she said without lifting her eyes from the grater on which she was grating cauliflowers to prepare stuffed *parathas* for dinner.

She would reach our house early in the morning. Her day started with the preparation of morning tea followed by other meals of the day. She was literally spoiling us by her unconditional services. By the time we got ready to leave for the day, steaming hot breakfast was laid on the table. Lunch was packed in our respective tiffin boxes that rested on the table for us. Working people like me, who have only toast and egg in their daily breakfast menu, know the value of getting fresh and delicious food every day. Lunch hour was no more a monotonous routine. Every day, I got an ecstatic feeling while removing the lid of the box to see one of my favourite dishes waiting to be eaten. In the evening, as soon as I reached home, she handed me a cup of refreshing lemon tea. Gradually I started feeling guilty for not paying her adequately for her services.

It was a lazy Sunday morning, the day of the week when Kamla pampered us with her special breakfast. Sundays were no restriction days, which gave her ample opportunity to impress us with her culinary skills. She was frying the vegetables for the cutlets when I went into the kitchen.

"I think I should increase your salary," I said.

"But why *Bhabhi*?"

"Because I had kept you only for preparing the meals, but you are here since morning cooking for us throughout the day. All the more, since Gita has decided to stay back and look after her inherited property in her village, I should raise your wages as now it is no more a stopgap arrangement."

"But *Bhabhi*, whatever you are paying is sufficient for me," she said. Suddenly she turned and held my hands in her palms. I could feel the tremble in her hands. She looked at me and spoke slowly as if someone was whispering in my ears.

"If you want to really help me, then please find my husband."

It seemed that someone had pushed me from the top of a mountain. Not even in my wildest dreams did I imagine that she would ask for this.

"But how can *I* find him? It would be better if you ask the police to find him," I said hurriedly, terrified by the newly imposed responsibility on my shoulders.

"I have done everything. Filed an FIR, published an ad in the newspaper, everything but got no response," she said and two drops of tears dropped on my hands which were still resting in her palms.

"Why did he leave you? Any idea?" I asked. This was the first time in last three weeks since she started working that we were talking about her husband. I could sense the reluctance in her voice the very first day while discussing about her husband, so never tried to create ripples in her life with these uncomfortable questions.

"I don't know *Bhabhi*. Maybe he didn't like me."

"But how can he leave you like this? You are his lawfully wedded wife," I said.

"But he left the other girl also, with whom he was living for the last one year."

Not able to decide whether to laugh at the situation or pull out hair from my scalp, I asked in dismay, "And you were okay with him staying with another girl?"

"It is very common in our society *Bhabhi*," she said, trying to make me understand how dutiful her husband was because he always fulfilled their (her baby's and her) needs and never left them alone to starve.

"So what on the earth could have happened that he left both of you suddenly? Did he find another girl?" trembling with anger and shock, I asked.

"No *Bhabhi*, he was very tense after he lost his job. It became very difficult for him to maintain two establishments," her voice was as calm as the morning sea.

Now this was the final blow that left me speechless for a few moments. I sat with a thump on the stool kept at the corner and looked at her innocent face. I was noticing that the vermilion she was putting in the partition of her hair was getting darker and denser with every passing day. Maybe this was the method this young, innocent girl had adopted to get her husband back.

The next morning Kamla brought a photograph of her husband and came to me as soon as she entered.

"*Bhabhi*, this is his photo. Please keep this with you. It might help you find him."

I looked at the man staring at me from the photo. He was a clean shaved man of about twenty five years with wheatish complexion. There was something in the expression of his eyes that made me feel uncomfortable even from behind the lenses of the camera. His looks didn't seem like that of a trustworthy person. The camera had also done a perfect job in capturing the shrewd cunning smile that peeped from the corner of his lips.

I took the picture and kept it in my handbag saying, "Okay, I'll see what I can do."

After about a week, Kamla came to me on Sunday with my morning tea. I took the tea and continued reading the newspaper. After a few seconds I noticed from the corner of the newspaper that she was still standing there, holding the empty tray.

"What happened? Want to say something?" I asked while folding the newspaper and keeping it on the center table.

"Yes," she said and sat on the floor.

"Did you get any information about *him*?" She never calls her husband by his name. In a world where women have even reached the space, she still believes in the age old norms that were set for women.

The matter had altogether skipped my mind amidst the daily hustle and bustle of life. A sudden wave of guilt hit me and I felt a lump in my throat.

"I am sorry. I completely forgot," trying to brush the feeling of guilt aside, I said in a little apologetic tone. "But don't worry. I promise I'll do something this week."

Her eyes sparkled and she left swiftly to prepare the breakfast. The food in the bowls had a special ingredient that day which made them extra delicious. Brimming with joy and hope, Kamla had made every effort to prepare everyone's favourite dish that day. For the very first time in these weeks, did I see her smiling and humming a song. I tried to recognise the song. It was a romantic song from an old Hindi movie.

I was astonished by the fact that she still loved her husband so much. Eagerly waiting for him, rarely did she miss any fast or *puja* to get him back. I was moved by her simplicity and the selfless love she bore for him that did not perish even after her husband had left her.

"Don't you feel cheated?" I had asked her once. "If he would have loved you, he wouldn't have left you."

"But he is my husband after all. See, only I have the right to wear this for him," she flaunted her *mangalsutra* with great pride in her eyes, as if it was the toughest medal to achieve in the world.

After handing over the photograph, she was fully assured that I will definitely find her husband. I had got his photograph published in every newspaper, gave ads in online media and circulated the picture in all social media channels. But every effort of mine was futile as even after two months, there was not a single clue about her husband. Initially every day she used to rush towards me as soon as I entered the house in the evening and ask, "*Bhabhi*, any news?" With nothing substantial to say and console her, I only nodded. Slowly and gradually she stopped asking about him. Now she only looked at me every day with great hope in her eyes when she saw me in the evening. There was something in her eyes that made me uncomfortable. At that moment I could do anything to get her husband back.

The National Science Conference was about to start in Delhi and I was invited there as a speaker to present a paper. My flight landed on time and I found Dr Shah, who had come to receive me, waiting at the airport. After having a cup of coffee, we drove towards the venue. Delhi has changed a lot in past few years. Earlier there were very few flyovers and foot over Bridges. But now after the Commonwealth Games and with the commencement of metro line services, the entire landscape of the city had got a magical touch. I have always loved the city and enjoyed my visits to the colourful capital of India. But during the past few visits I have felt that the crowd was increasing with every passing day. The land of opportunities has invited many youngsters from other cities of the country, which was gradually pushing the city towards a population explosion. However, all these factors could not diminish the charm of this wonderful city.

I was reading my mails on my phone when the car stopped with a jerk. I looked out of the window to see the huge assembly of vehicles of every size waiting for the green signal. Small vendors started gathering near the vehicles to attract the attention of the people. Books, toys, window shields, balloons, one can buy all sorts of things at these traffic signals of Delhi. Suddenly a group of eunuchs passed my car. There were eight to ten eunuchs in the group who were clapping sharply and asking for money from every passer-by.

Dr Shah said, "These eunuchs are real nuisance madam. There is no crime that these people do not commit. You will be surprised to learn that most of these are actually healthy males who have joined these groups to earn easy money."

Disgusted by the feeling of how much a person can stoop down to earn money, I looked out and my eyes fell on the eunuch standing at the corner of the window of my car. It seemed I had seen this person earlier. Draped in a bright pink sari, wearing shiny cheap jewellery and loud makeup, he was producing deafening sound with his sharp claps and unsynchronised songs along with his group members. Trying hard to recollect where had I seen this person earlier, I felt an electric shock passing my body. It was him. I never forget faces. It could not be anyone else. It was Kamla's husband. He was looking at me with the same shrewd look like the one in his photograph. Realising I was staring at him, he started coming towards me to beg for money with a smile. And that was the final stamp that sealed my conclusion. It was confirmed. No other person on the earth had the capacity to smile with such cunningness.

My car moved because the signal had turned green and with that my mind also travelled back to Lucknow. Two innocent faces flashed in front of my eyes. Kamla's son must have started crawling on his knees by now. In another few months he will start talking. Who will come and hold his hands along with Kamla when he will stumble while learning to walk? When he will cry for his father, who will come and hold the little one in his arms? And Kamla? She is still waiting for her husband to come back and look after her and her child. She comes to me with her questioning eyes filled with hope every day when I come home. Will I be able to face her the next time she comes and asks me about her husband? When I was leaving for Delhi, she had said when she learned about my tour, "*Bhabhi*, I have heard very fine jewellery is available in Delhi."

"Hmm, so?"

"Can you bring a nice *bichiya* (toe ring) for me from Delhi? It's *Karva chauth* next week and I want to wear it and pray for my husband's return on that day," she had said with a thousand hopes in her eyes.

I felt like getting down from the car and shouting at the top of my voice "Kamla, this wait has no end. No *bichiya* or *Karva chauth* can bring your husband back. He is now part of an entirely different society. Forget him. He will never come back." But words failed me and hung like an awkward lull at the base of my throat. Will I ever be able to tell her what I had seen in Delhi? What will I say to her when she will ask me about him?

She had said, "*Bhabhi*, don't forget to bring my *bichiya*. I know this year God will have mercy on me. My *Karva chauth* offering will not fail this year."

I felt a lump in my throat by recalling her gleeful smile. Her eyes held so much promise and hope that the only question that plagued me now was, will I ever be able to tell her the truth? Will I?

Story 8: The Second Tsunami

The sky was a brilliant blue that day. The waves softly crashed onto the shore almost poetically. It was the kind of silence that happened before a storm. And, what a storm it was. The waves took everyone by surprise and before anyone knew, they left nothing but devastation in their wake. They sent people running for cover while thousands were drowned in their watery graves. Chaos broke and people ran to whichever place they could stay safely.

While some looked helplessly for loved ones, rest were running to find a safer place to shelter themselves, frightened and perplexed by the sight of huge demonic waves. They were proceeding towards the city to engulf it along with its habitat and had now started swallowing whole fishing villages and towns killing thousands of people living in those areas.

Little Padma was returning from school holding the fingers of her younger brother Anuj, when the tragedy hit the city. Anuj had just started going to the school and Padma had gleefully accepted the position of an elder sister along with its duties and responsibilities. They were returning from the beach side when suddenly the huge waves started coming towards them. It was a frightening scene and both of them were dumbstruck for a moment. Everywhere there were people running and shouting making it difficult to hear anything clearly. Unable to comprehend the situation, Padma held Anuj's hand and started running along with the other people, dragging him behind her.

She was trying to pull Anuj with all her might but after a while it became overbearing for a young girl of ten years to bear the weight of her five year old brother. She was running with heavy breath and felt as if her heart will leap out at her mouth. But within all this pain, she didn't let go of the grip on Anuj's hands at any cost. Finally when they reached the safe zone, they were panting profusely and had reached a semi-conscious state due to the exertion and sudden shock.

After some time, the terrifying show of the huge water walls calmed down after causing mass destruction. Many houses and lives were washed away with the waves. Dead bodies along with other objects like chairs, sofas, beds, utensils, etc., were floating on the water, sometimes going under water and then coming up. Houses, cars, trees, boats… everything was crumpled, uprooted, pulverized and destroyed. The tragedy had also left many people homeless, many children orphaned and a series of tragic sagas behind it. Padma's parents along with all their belongings were also washed away by the huge fierce waves.

The storm left everyone with a big heaviness in the hearts and a feeling of great shock and sadness. Padma and Anuj were also in a state of shock and it was difficult to say whether they would survive at all. Padma, unaware of the cruel act of fate, was looking everywhere in great anticipation for her parents but every part of the area disappointed her. Anuj was too young to realise the seriousness of the situation. He kept crying for his parents. But little Padma? She could gauge how disastrous the storm had been and was constantly praying for her parents to be safe. She remembered how her mother, gorgeously dressed in silk saris and wearing shining gold ornaments, was always immersed in her prayers and religious ceremonies. Every morning and evening she sang beautiful verses of holy Ramayana while praying to the Gods. She often told little Padma, "If you pray to God, the biggest demons run away in fear!" And to drive the demon away and bring her parents back, she was praying, praying to be with her loved ones again.

It had been quite long since she had found any food to eat and now she was getting frequent stomach cramps. She looked all around but could not find any familiar face to whom she could go and ask for help. Her mind went back to the time when her mother used to run after Anuj and her to finish the glass of milk. Her eyes got wet with the thought of how her mother used to beseech her to eat another small portion of rice even after she was full. Stressed, tired and hungry, she was sitting at one corner, quietly watching the dreadful scene and praying for help and her parents to arrive soon.

Aid had started arriving but the pace was very slow as everybody was in a state of shock. Several volunteers, medical and police teams had started reaching out for help and rescue too, but they were also in an utterly confused state, unable to decide where to start. They were trying to gauge the situation to decide where to go and which specific work to start with. All around there were heaps of debris from destroyed houses. Many people were arriving with food packets, clean water and medicines, clothes and tents but people in need of the help always outnumbered the amount of help that arrived. Those who were lucky were shifted to tents but there were many who were waiting for a temporary roof on their heads.

People flocked to get the relief items and those with greater muscle power triumphed in grabbing the help. Little Padma tried several times but every time she was pushed behind by the huge and maddening crowd and was left with no choice other than to watch them with moist eyes grabbing the food packets, blankets and other items.

Suddenly Padma was promoted from the role of a sister to the role of a mother. All of a sudden they were exposed to the harsh tragedies of life, left all alone to struggle for their survival among the crowd of ruthless and heartless people. There was no one to take care of these kids who had lost the cosy warm shelter of their home along with the love and care of their parents. Sitting on the bare ground, she was recalling the secure atmosphere of her home. Anuj was utterly terrified and shocked by the incident and could not understand what was happening around him. At times he was crying for his parents and rest of the times, he was following Padma everywhere she went while holding the corner of her skirt.

It was the second day after the Tsunami and little Padma could manage to get only one blanket and a small packet of biscuit. Anuj, trying to bear the burning fire inside his stomach, could not dare to enter the crowd and kept standing at a corner staring at the devastated people. Padma tried hard but failed to get hold of another packet of biscuit. She looked at the size of the small packet in her hand and turned to her brother. Her eyes dampened with the sight of Anuj who was staring at the packet with a sudden twinkle in his eyes with the thought of eating something after two days. She slowly handed over the packet to him forgetting about her stomach cramps. She had grown overnight and was ready to sacrifice everything for her brother.

Days passed and Padma kept on performing the role of a mother perfectly, until her belly, the ungrateful wretch ditched her. Trying to satisfy the monstrous demon called hunger inside her brother's belly, she had totally forgotten about the one she was carrying inside her. It was another day in the camp when everyone was waiting for the food van. Unable to bear the pain in her stomach any more, she ran towards the van when it arrived with the bread packets.

For the first time, she was running to get the food for herself. The thought of her hungry younger brother had totally vaporised. People toppled over each other in the race of getting the bread and the most she could manage was a small bun.

Anuj came running towards her and jumped towards her hands to grab the bun. Padma instantly lifted her hand to take the bun out of Anuj's reach. Hunger had overpowered the love for her brother and for the first time she pushed him on the ground with her left hand.

"No, I will eat this," she cried aloud.

"Didi, bun," Anuj repeated the words as he struggled between Padma's hands and feet to grab the piece. The resistance from Padma was increasing with the growing pain in her belly due to the hunger cramps. Finally, unable to calm her little brother, Padma caught hold of him from the neck with both her hands and shook him, shouting, "I will eat this. Do you understand? This is for ME!"

Anuj struggled for a while but soon his hands and feet became numb and dropped, lifeless. Padma, relieved by her brother's acceptance, made him lie down beside her on the floor and covered his body with the only blanket they had got from the volunteers. She took out the bun from her pocket and took a bite, patting Anuj's head softly to make him sleep, unaware of the fact that a second Tsunami called *hunger* had engulfed her brother.

Story 9: The Example

I looked around the huge hall from the dais and found it fully packed with lecturers, professors and other staff members of the university. The vice chancellor was speaking at the podium, thanking me for my unprecedented contribution towards the education system. Every eye was on me that day–some with admiration, some with professional jealousy and some were looking at me vacantly, waiting for the speech to be over. The praise, the accolades and the thanking speeches that were showered on me could have filled anybody with pride, but there was something that was troubling me. Every word of the praise was lost in the huge vacuum that had enveloped me. A sense of non-fulfilment was pinching me every moment and a deep dark hollowness had engulfed me. A successful career of thirty five years as a professor and principal of a reputed college has not been able to fill the void that I was experiencing within me. Today, on the day of my retirement, when I look back at the past years, I am unable to recall a single event that can make me feel content with my life. The all praise farewell speeches, the long list of awards and the recognitions, everything seemed to be mocking me.

After the party was over, the new principal accompanied me to drop me home in the official vehicle. Throughout the drive back home, I was so engrossed in my thoughts, I could hardly converse with my successor. My thoughts came to a halt when the car stopped at the entrance of my home.

"Good day Sir, now I will take your leave," he said before leaving, extending his hand for a handshake. "Please keep guiding us in continuing the job you have started."

I nodded with a feeble smile and shook hands with him. I tried to say something but words choked my throat. Overwhelmed by emotions, I stood there like a statue and the car moved. I kept staring at it until it faded out of sight. I looked at the long empty road and felt a heavy weight crush my chest. Walking slowly, I came inside with heavy feet and dumped myself on the sofa. The room was full of bouquets and gifts that were the certificates of my achievements, yet I felt my hands were empty with nothing to look back to in my life. "What is so great about these thirty five years of my journey as a teacher?" I thought, but there was no one to give me the answer.

I don't know how long I kept sitting like that, staring at the ceiling of the room. The sun was going to set in a couple of minutes and had filled the whole sky with its golden radiance mixed with shades of grey. It seemed as if it was trying to shine one last time with all its might before ending the day. I felt a strange connection with the pale sunlight that filled the room that was gradually diminishing, filling the room with a hollow darkness.

Suddenly the doorbell shrieked and I got up with a jolt to open the door. I found a smart young lady in her mid-thirties, standing there with a beautiful bouquet in her hands. Draped in a light blue sari with hair tucked neatly behind her ears, this lady had a strange sparkle in her large beautiful eyes.

"Congratulations sir," she said extending the bouquet towards me. "Congratulations for the new innings of your life," she said with a broad smile. Despite ransacking my memories, I failed to accomplish the simple task of recognising this confident young lady and I stood there still, looking at her with inquiring eyes.

"Sir, can you recognise me?" she asked again.

"Well, umm...," I muttered.

"I am Abhilasha Sir, BSc. IInd Year, the sleeping girl?"

A long pause...

"How would you remember me Sir! I am not the only one whose life has changed because of you," she sighed.

I tried one last time and suddenly it felt as if someone hit me hard on my head with a hammer. An innocent but sad face of a young girl flashed in front of my eyes. I moved away slowly from the entrance making way for her. Putting the flowers in the vase kept in the corner of the room, she asked me,

"Sir, you look tired. Shall I make coffee for you?"

My maid, who is the only support system of my bachelor life, was on weekly off that day. So the offer was like a godsend for me. I nodded in affirmation and sat down on the sofa, closing my eyes.

This girl took me back fifteen years, when I was working as a Chemistry faculty in an eminent college in Pune. Only the most brilliant students backed by several top ranks in studies as well as other co-curricular activities could pass the stringent admission process and qualify to get education in the college. Abhilasha was also among the lucky few to get admission. Nothing remarkable happened in the first year. But from the beginning of the second year, this girl's behaviour and academic progress reminded the management every day about their misjudgement of giving her admission in the college.

A sudden sleeping disorder seemed to hit the girl and every day she was caught sleeping during the lectures on the last bench when all the other long wooden benches were occupied by attentive students. Gradually the whole college came to know about the girl, who by this time had earned the name, *"The Sleeping Girl."*

Fuming with the indiscipline that was cropping up among the students due to this girl, I called her one day in my room. She came and stood at the door without saying a word. I looked up from the book kept on the table in front of me and found her standing at the entrance, staring at the floor.

"Come in," I said. Slowly she came inside and stood in front of me with both of her hands crossed in front of her.

"Do you have any idea why I have called you here?" I asked her.

She nodded.

"Any explanations...?" No answer.

"I am talking to you! Why do you always sleep during the lectures? Do you know you can be thrown out of here if you continue like this?"

"I am sorry, Sir," she said with her face down, looking at the floor.

"Okay, this is the last warning. If you continue sleeping during the lectures, you will be suspended from the college."

"Thank you and sorry, Sir," she said and left the room.

Throughout the day, the strange desolate look that she wore on her face followed me. There was definitely some story that she had very carefully locked behind her silence. The thought of learning more about this girl kept creeping into my mind but soon they took a backseat and my daily routine took over.

The first term examination results were out and they painted her report sheet in red. The news broke like wildfire and the whole college was aghast as this girl had created history in the college by failing the examinations. The exasperated principal was pulling his hair out fearing the reputation of the college that was at stake due to the historical performance of Abhilasha. Considering the seriousness of the matter, he called for a joint meeting to decide the fate of the girl. Everyone who attended the meeting was in favour of her suspension and I was the only one who was hesitating in slaughtering the poor girl without giving her a chance. The lonely desolate look on her face prevented me from being so harsh on this girl. Her first year results in front of me were creating a contrasting picture of her. How could I believe that anyone who is so sharp and bright to get distinction marks in the first year can turn dumb overnight? There is some mystery and I must find it out, I thought.

After long discussions and continuous persuasions with the board, I was able to save this girl from direct suspension. The principal agreed to grant me time till the half-yearly results and made it very clear that the girl will be out of the college if she fails even in a single paper during the half-term exams.

Determined to act as a mentor instead of a teacher, I decided to change the fate of a promising young girl whose life was on the verge of vanquish. In the evening my determination took me to her house and I was standing at the doorstep pressing the bell. When the door opened, she jumped with surprise to see me in front of it. It took her a while to come to terms and after a couple of minutes she invited me inside. I looked around the house and found it to be a small room where there were only four chairs and a study table that were kept in a corner. A small cot was kept in the other corner, which was neatly covered by a cotton sheet. I walked in and sat on one of the chairs. Abhilasha quietly followed me and stood beside me.

"Do you know why have I come here?" I looked up at her and asked.

"No," she said with a confused look at her face.

"To discuss about your progress in the studies during last few months," I continued.

She didn't say anything and looked at me with a strange look. It was very difficult to describe the expression in her eyes that was a mix of helplessness, sorrow and sense of failure. I noticed that amidst all the conversation, Abhilasha was looking at her wristwatch again and again.

"Are you going out somewhere?" I asked.

"Yes sir, my shift starts at seven in the evening and the cab will be here any moment," she replied.

"You work somewhere?" Now this was news to me. I did not know that Abhilasha had been working somewhere. But whatever on earth had made her work at such a young age?

"Yes, in a call center," she said.

"But why?" I couldn't help the pitch of my voice from rising. Dejected by the fact she was more interested in her job than building her career, I asked again, "How can your parents allow you to work at this tender age? This is the time for you to concentrate on your studies."

The moment I said this, she burst into tears covering her face with her palms. Taken aback by her reaction, I jumped of my chair. Not able to comprehend the situation and find the right words to soothe her, I stood still beside her, mute, watching her cry. After a couple of minutes she stopped crying and looked at me after wiping her tears with her hands.

"I am sorry sir," she said in a soft voice. Her face was looking dull while few drops of tears were still shining on her eyelashes.

"It's okay Abhilasha, don't be sorry," I said and after a little pause I asked, "Do you want to share your problems with me? Maybe I can help?"

I again walked to the chair and sat on it waiting patiently for her to speak. She pulled another chair and sat in front of me. She started her story and when she finished I felt for a few seconds as if the whole world was spinning around me.

They were a happy family of three people…Abhilasha and her parents who belonged to that stratum of the society that does not have much income to boast of and family is their only asset. Pampered but not spoilt, Abhilasha was the apple of their eyes. She was a bright student and her parents took every pain for providing her everything that could help her achieve great heights in her life. Everything was going fine when fate snatched all the happiness from this family. On one dark night when her parents were returning from the market, a truck smashed into them, leaving Abhilasha all alone in this big bad world. She felt as if the world around her has crashed down. This was just the beginning of Abhilasha's miseries. All the relatives fled, deserting her, and she was left alone on her own. With time when she could manage to collect the pieces of her shattered self, Abhilasha jumped into the battle of life to fulfil the dreams of her parents. She joined a job at a call center to support herself and continue her studies. But the night shift job was claiming a huge price from her. She was left with very little time to sleep and concentrate on her studies. Now the reason of her sleeping during the lectures was no mystery for me.

It was a little too much for an eighteen year old girl. There was a long pause and the atmosphere was getting heavy with silence. I was stirred deep within by the cruel joke played by life on this young girl. Words were struggling to come out of my mouth. Unable to find any suitable words, I slowly got up, walked to her and put my hands on her head.

"Abhilasha," I said. She looked at me with her eyes full of tears. "Don't worry. I'll see to it that you complete your education." It was her inner power that kept her struggling and now it got transferred within me that prompted in my ears, "She is a brave girl fighting alone with the tragedy. You must do something for her." She did not say anything, only looked at me with grateful eyes.

It was now my turn to fight the battle as getting a second year student appointed as a lab trainee definitely raises many eyebrows. The authorities were strictly against my decision but Abhilasha's innocent face filled me with a certain inner strength that kept me going. Finally I succeeded in convincing everyone and when I handed over the letter to Abhilasha, she was speechless. The stipend was enough to support her monetarily. She could now leave her night shift job and continue her studies.

On the day of half-yearly results, the same anxiety was creeping within me that had filled me during my student days. Finally the results were announced and both of us came out triumphant. Abhilasha had topped the charts. Fifteen years have passed since then. Gradually the incident faded from my memory.

I was sitting in the same position when Abhilasha entered the room with a tray and the room got filled with the aroma of fresh coffee. She came towards me and I picked one of the two mugs kept on the tray.

"Thanks," I said.

"So what are you doing now?"

"Working as a chemistry lecturer in Nagpur University," she said and smiled.

"Hmm...very good. Are you happy?" I also smiled.

"Very happy sir. Thank you for everything you have done for me," she said.

"But what have I done in this? It's all your hard work and determination that has helped you achieve your goals."

"No sir, I don't know for how long I could have continued like that if you wouldn't have come like an angel. I owe everything to you sir. You gave a direction to my life."

She got up, put a silk shawl around my shoulder and bent to touch my feet. The moment was overwhelming for me. Suddenly I felt a heavy weight lift off my chest. My life didn't seem so meaningless after all. Of all the medals that I had got in my life, this was the best award that I had received on my retirement day.

By now it had become quite dark. She got up and switched on the light. The bright yellow light of the bulb filled the whole room, illuminating everything around me. Now everything was bright, clear and cheerful. Abhilasha had given me the meaning of my life. She answered the question which had been troubling me all this while. I was satisfied that my life was not wasted and I made a difference to someone's life even if it was just one student.

The farewell speech, the garland, the applause... everything seemed fake until this girl stood in front of me like a live example of my contribution towards life. Perhaps I was waiting for an example. How could I believe anything unless explained with examples? After all I am a person of science, and science doesn't accept anything without proof or examples. Isn't it?

Story 10: The Meeting

Payal stirred the simmering curry for a while and continued slicing the cucumber to prepare the salad.

She would have to hurry as it was already noon and Ria would be there any moment. She wanted to be free before her childhood friend arrived to have lunch with her, whom she was going to meet after twenty five long years. Payal was excited by the thought that she will be meeting Ria after so long. Referred to as twins by everyone in the colony as well as in the school despite the fact that they did not have any blood relation, they were always seen together going to school, doing homework, playing and wouldn't have minded sleeping together if their parents had allowed them.

Payal wanted to plan a perfect meeting to welcome her friend and unable to figure out how to do it, she finally decided to show her love for Ria through her culinary art. And all these preparations were just a part of her idea of a perfect welcome treat. She had been busy since morning preparing the long list of delicacies that once used to be Ria's favourite. She picked a spoon and tasted a spoonful of the *matar paneer* curry that was simmering on the stove and the taste of the curry brought a smile on her face. After pouring it in the special chinabone bowl she went to the dining room to keep it on the table along with the other bowls, every one of which was filled with a special delicacy, waiting to be relished by the honourable guest of the day.

It was Ria's mother who had inspired Payal to learn the skill. Whenever she visited them, a new dish was served to her along with the task of guessing the main ingredient.

Thrilled by tasting a new dish every second day and the fun filled game of guessing its main ingredient, Payal had decided at a very young age to master the art. And in these twenty five years, she has done perfect justice to the promise that she had made to herself several years back.

Memories of the days spent with Ria brought a smile on Payal's face and she started opening the lid of every bowl to ensure that every dish was worthy enough to add the accolade on her shoulder. One vital truth that her mastered art had taught her was that people rely on a plethora of sensory inputs when they eat. It is not only the taste that plays the vital role in deciding the fate of any dish. They first smell the aroma of the steaming curry, then eat the dish with their eyes and integrate all these information before actually putting it in their mouth. And this is the reason she had taken every care to make the dishes taste as well as look good. Heaving a sigh of extreme satisfaction, she saw the display of the art that had earned her the most appreciation in her life and looked up at the clock. It showed 12:30 pm.

She rushed to her bedroom and quickly scanned the wardrobe. Considering the hot sweltering weather outside, she took out a simple lemon-coloured cotton *bandhej salwar-kameez*. As it is Delhi summers are horrible, especially during the months of May and June. To match the summer moods of the city, one needs to choose the fabric and dress very carefully so as to not mess with the heat that is poured ruthlessly by the sun. Besides that her profession as a teacher had also taught her how to dress elegantly with minimal accessories.

Payal had always believed that the happiness of life lies in the small pleasures that all of us are blessed with. But Ria was just the opposite and had always dreamt large. Aspiring for a lavish lifestyle, she was never interested in the simple, tiny yet beautiful moments of life. But this contrast in their basic nature had never pushed them apart.

Lost in the memories of the days spent with Ria during her schooldays, she brushed her waist long hair and tied it into a ponytail. Giving the final touches to her makeup with a dash of face powder and a black bindi on her forehead, she looked at her image in the mirror and smiled with admiration.

As the time of Ria's arrival neared, her heart started beating very fast. To kill time, she picked a magazine from the bookrack, went to the hall and sat on the sofa, carelessly flipping the pages of the book. It seemed as if the moments refused to pass and when she looked at the clock hanging at the wall again, it was only 12:50 pm. She wondered and looked at her wristwatch to check if the time shown by the clock was right.

"This is so unlikely of Ria. She used to be so punctual earlier," Payal thought and got up from the sofa and stood at the window from where the main street was clearly visible. Unable to locate any traces of her friend, Payal started wandering in the thoughts about her teenage days again.

Both of them were living in the same colony and their admission in the same school strengthened their friendship further. They used to share every secret with each other. When on her eighteenth birthday, Ria was celebrating the day with her new boyfriend, Payal was handling the situation in front of her parents. Ria also never disappointed Payal in her friendship and when she lost her file just one day before her practical examination, it was Ria who burnt midnight oil to complete the file again for her.

Such a friendship came to an abrupt pause when Payal's father got transferred to Chennai. It seemed to both of them as if the world has come to an end. And when the day arrived when Payal's family was shifting to Chennai, both of them kept crying for a good two hours, holding each other's hand. Finally after making a promise of writing a letter every week, both of them bid goodbye to each other with eyes full of tears. In the beginning the frequency of writing letters was weekly; it gradually turned to monthly, then yearly and finally the exchange of letters between them ceased. With the passage of time, both of them got busy in their new life with new friends.

Just two days back, Payal learned about Ria being in the same city through a common friend. Ecstatic to learn about her friend, Payal did not waste a moment to take Ria's number and call her. She feared if time had faded her from Ria's memory, but she jumped over the phone as she listened to her voice.

An invitation for a lunch at her place seemed to be the most appropriate thing for Payal to do to welcome her friend for the first time after all these years. Being an expert cook, arranging lunch parties was a child's play for her and she also wanted to impress her friend with her art.

"Seems your friend is really special," her husband had said in the morning with a mischievous smile on his face when he saw Payal pulling out the special sets of tablemats and cushion covers from the cupboard. Payal lifted her eyes from the cushion and smiled at her husband and continued putting the covers on the cushions. These covers enjoyed a special status in their house. Payal always used these to impress and welcome her most special guests. She wanted this meeting to be a perfect one where both of them could relive their teenage days.

After waiting for about half an hour, finally Payal caught the sight of a black Audi stopping in front of her house.

She rushed to open the door and came out running to welcome Ria. The chauffeur opened the door and Ria stepped out of the car. A beautiful fragrance of an expensive perfume filled the whole atmosphere. Payal wanted to hug her friend tight but her extended arms dropped automatically when they were answered by a mere "Hi."

Dressed in designer items from head to toe, Ria was looking stunning and could give a tough competition to any model.

"This area is so congested; it took my driver more than an hour to locate your house," Ria wrinkled her nose and said.

Payal had not dreamt in her wildest dream that their conversation will start with these words. It seemed someone hit her hard on her chest but she quickly controlled her emotions and holding hands of Ria, took her inside and asked her to sit in front of the cooler. Hot red sun was glowing outside, burning with its rays everything that came in their path. And this torture of the sun had also crept into their house; they were trying to battle it with the cooler kept in the room.

"Don't you have an AC?" Ria asked with a certain amount of disgust on her face. Payal felt as if Ria thrashed her with a stick every time she opened her mouth.

"No, we cannot afford one. Actually we have several other priorities. Both our kids are staying in hostels to study engineering," Payal said in a low voice.

"Oh, but you know, I can't even imagine living without an AC."

Without saying anything, Payal smiled and handed over a glass of ice-cold water to Ria. Ria kept the empty glass on the table and arranged the *pallu* of her designer off-white and pink sari over her spotless manicured arms. Taking out a handkerchief from her purse, she started fanning herself with it. With every passing moment, a portion of Payal's excitement was dying inside her.

"So? How's life going?" Payal asked.

"Rocking," Ria said and flaunted her designer sari when she realised Payal had not noticed her expensive attire. "Actually you know I was dying to meet you and bought this Satya Paul sari just for this meeting."

"Oh! It's nice," Payal looked at the sari casually and replied.

"Thanks! Hey you still wear a ponytail?" Ria said again without realising Payal was waiting for her to recall their earlier days they had spent together. "Why don't you get these cut in the latest style?" she continued.

"I am happy the way I am."

"But you must do something about your dressing style. You look so plain in these kind of *salwar suits*."

Ria's statement again took Payal back to her teenage days when both of them died to get hold of any handloom dress. They had to travel all the way to the town from their campus, which was twenty five kilometres away to buy any stuff from the emporium. She still remembers how she had to toil in the markets with Ria for one whole day to find a green and red *bandhej dupatta* for her–just like the one a famous Bollywood actress had worn in a popular movie. It was Ria's words when she finally got hold of the *dupatta*–"You know Payal? These handlooms never go out of fashion. We can even wear this after twenty five years!" Payal thought and looked at her yellow cotton *salwar-kameez*.

Today, this Ria seemed to be someone else who had no memories left from their teenage days. Is this what they had met to discuss after so many years?

Ria took out a packet and gave it to Payal saying, "I got this perfume specially for you. This is the latest French collection. Though the price was very high but I bought it for you because I knew you will love the fragrance."

Payal felt a large lump in her throat, and disgusted with the display of her designer labels and unwarranted comments on her dressing style, she got up thanking for the gift and asked, "Shall we have lunch? It's already very late."

"Oh, yeah sure," Ria said with a bit of disappointment noticing Payal's lukewarm response to the expensive gift. Payal laid the table and waited for a word of appreciation from Ria about the variety of food items that she had specially prepared for her. But Ria quietly pulled a chair and sat down.

"Please don't give me much. I don't eat all this oily food you know," she said placing her hand over the plate when Payal tried to put the second *poori* on it.

"I hope your health is fine?" Payal asked, worrying over Ria's health.

"Oh yeah. I am perfectly alright. But you know, I have stopped eating these Indian dishes. They are full of oil," she said and pushed the bowl of *nargisi kofta* away that once used to be her favourite. The smile on Payal's face vanished but she controlled her emotions and pulled a chair for herself. Yearning to talk about how the years had passed without each other, Payal asked again, "Did you ever think about me?"

"Oh! Many times!" Ria said tearing the *poori* with her long manicured nails. "You know when we went to Paris for the first time, I was reminded of you… how you always wanted to see *Mona Lisa* in the *Louvre.*"

"You have seen it?" Payal's eyes widened at the mention of *Mona Lisa.*

"Yes, several times. And last year when we went on a Europe tour, my husband got me this diamond necklace," Ria tried to dazzle Payal's eyes again with the shine of her necklace. But Payal was looking for something else in Ria. She was trying to find her friend who had got buried under designer labels and expensive jewellery. In front of her was a lady who was busy in displaying her wealth from the moment she had arrived. Payal's world revolved around her family. She was happy in her two-bedroom flat, leading a simple life with her husband and kids. Never interested in branded items, she cherished the simple moments of life.

Payal had so many questions churning within that she wanted to ask Ria. She had so many things to share with her friend that had happened in last quarter of century but now her friend was lost somewhere. Disappointed, Payal tried once again.

"Are you working somewhere? And what are your kids doing?" she asked.

"No way. I am the wife of an established businessman and don't need to work you know."

"Well really? As far as I remember it was you who was always in the favour of women working for self-growth and independence," Payal thought to herself but did not say anything.

"And my kids are in school and enjoying life. After all their father is earning in millions," Ria said with great pride and joy.

The display of wealth was overflowing from every sentence that Ria spoke, which was making Payal all the more irritable. The sizzle of meeting her old friend had already died down earlier and now she started feeling suffocated with a sudden feeling of detest cropping up inside her. Nothing was happening as expected and now she wanted this meeting to end. When the lunch got over, Ria looked at her watch. "I will have to leave now. I have to get to a kitty party," she said and looked at the cooler. Payal felt a wave of emotion engulf her when she learned the real reason of Ria leaving so early. She went inside and returned with a packet in her hand and gave it to Ria.

"Oh! Why did you bother about all these things?" Ria said and started opening the gift. A dazzling rose-gold and silver watch was lying inside a box. "Titan? But you know, I no longer use these Indian brands," she said and wagged her wrist in front of Payal's eyes that was adorned by a beautiful Rado watch. Ria kept the watch in the box and put it on the table and said, "You keep this with you. Unnecessarily it will be wasted if I take it with me. You may use it later on." Payal felt as if Ria had slapped hard on her face. Shocked, she could not find any words to say.

Ria got up and said, "Thanks for everything Payal. I shall take your leave now. Keep in touch," and headed towards the front door. Payal mechanically raised her hand to say goodbye, entirely disappointed by the meeting. Her every effort to welcome Ria and entertain her had gone unrecognised by Ria who was once a friend of hers. Hoping never to meet again, both of them said goodbye to each other and turned back. The meeting had separated these twins after twenty five years with an invisible surgery.

Story 11: Mirage

It was a lazy Sunday morning. The sunlight peeked in through my drapes, casually playing with my face. I pulled up the covers to have another short nap. The night earlier was very hectic due to an official meeting and my whole body was still aching and my eyes were still heavy. I was on my way to wander in the world of dreams again when my plan of not leaving the bed for another hour was destroyed by the aroma of freshly prepared coffee that suddenly filled the room. I peeked from the corner of the cover to see the mug that my mother had just kept on the side table. For a few moments I struggled with the aroma of the coffee but finally surrendered and got up on the bed. I picked up the cup and took a small sip of the steaming hot coffee, feeling the warm sunrays on my face. The tall moringa trees had started blooming and the view of the small white flowers among the green leaves was filling me with a serene freshness. I was enjoying every moment of it when suddenly the clock struck nine. I jumped out of my bed. How could I forget my mother was going to meet her sister today and I must free her up by twelve noon?

Taking out the towel from the wardrobe, I quickly went towards the washroom. The sound of utensils was coming from the kitchen downstairs where my mother was preparing the breakfast while humming a song softly. Suddenly I got hit by a strong feeling of detest that filled my mouth with a strange bitterness. The soft melodious song appeared to be the loudest noise in the world to me and I wondered how someone can behave so normally after ruining her daughter's life.

"Khushi, *beta* breakfast is ready. Come quickly," she called from the kitchen and I banged the door of the washroom, murmuring, "Huh! Don't know how she can show fake love with such perfection."

After the shower, the bitterness was washed away to a certain extent and I started feeling light and fresh. When I entered the dining room, I realised how hungry I was after seeing steaming hot *poha* and filter coffee on the table–it was my favourite and I could eat potful of this delicious dish. My mother served me a plateful of *poha* and asked while pouring the coffee in a mug, "Will you go to buy the ticket today?"

"Hmm," I said, putting a spoonful of *poha* in my mouth, not wanting to extend the conversation further. I get a choking feeling while talking to her and have always believed that she doesn't deserve nice behaviour from me. Though this has never discouraged her from showing love and care towards me.

After the breakfast, I hurriedly slipped on my sandal and stepped out of the house looking at my watch. "Oh my God. It's already 10:30 am! I need to rush to reach there before 11:00 am," I thought and walked quicker to reach the market before the ticket counter was closed. I could not afford to miss the chance of buying the tickets for weekly draw, which is the only hope of my life. After my father, it was me who was continuing the practice started by him, and it has now become an important part of my life.

Sundays have always been special for me, when my father used to take me to the market for buying the ticket of weekly lucky draw. During the walk to the market, he used to tell me how he will be spending the money when he wins a jackpot. "Khushi, you'll see one day I WILL win the jackpot and that will be the happiest day of my life."

I used to wander in a dreamland while listening to him, imagining the things that we would do after winning the lottery. My father had always wanted to lead a lavish and extravagant life and it was only the prize money that could get him his dream lifestyle. His salary provided us a decent life but my father's dreams were too big.

With the thought of my father, a smile came on my face. The moments spent with him started flashing in front of my eyes like a film. In the first scene I was sitting on his lap listening to an interesting story. Then the scene changed and I was going to the market holding his hands to buy my favourite sweets and candies. The scenes kept changing and I relived the eight years of my life that I had spent with my father.

The last scene put a sudden brake on my thoughts and small beads of sweat started appearing on my forehead. I still remember the day when he returned from office and told me about his transfer to another city.

"No, you can't go without me," I shouted and started crying aloud, yelling and thumping the floor with my foot.

"Khushi, try to understand. It is about my job. I have to follow the orders," he said, taking me into his arms and trying to calm me.

"No, I don't know anything. I cannot live without you. Take us with you," I said while crying at the top of my voice.

Amidst all this, we could not notice two large eyes, filled with tears, looking at us quietly. My father kept cajoling me and my mother went inside, without saying a word.

I was shattered after my father left and felt as if something had died within me. A huge void started growing inside me and there was no one I could share my agony with.

My mother had always been indifferent towards us and at the tender age of eight, it was not difficult for me to understand the fact that it was my mother who was responsible for my father's disinterest towards the family. She never accompanied us to any picnic or outing. Whenever I needed her, she was either busy in office or other household jobs.

"Mamma, will you take me to the market to buy ice cream?" I asked her one day after my father was gone, while doing my homework.

"Khushi, see how much work is left to be completed?" she put down the vegetables on the table that she was cutting and looked up at me. "This is the time for you to study. So be a good girl and complete your homework. We'll have the ice cream on Sunday."

Now how could I tell her that I wanted to have the ice cream now. Now means now. Not Sunday. On Sunday I wanted to go to the fun park and have lots of candyfloss and popcorn like I used to do with my father. But I knew it was useless to ask again, so I continued doing my homework. The next Sunday, my mother came to my room in the morning and sat on the bed beside me saying, "Come on Khushi. Get up quickly. We are going to the fun park today." She was running her hand through my hair but every time she touched me, I was filled with a strange feeling. Perhaps I was still sulking over the ice cream incident and had not forgiven her for it. I removed her hand from my head and said, "Let me sleep. I don't want to go anywhere."

She kept looking at my face for a couple of moments and then slowly left the room. Gradually this became a usual affair. At times she was busy and sometimes I pretended to be busy. I pulled back my hands every time she extended her hands towards me. Eventually the gap between us increased to such a level that I created an imaginative world of mine and started living in it with my father. In this beautiful world of mine, there was no space for my mother. I could not forgive her for my father leaving us behind.

Sundays and holidays became the most dreadful punishments for me when I had to spend the whole day with my mother. The only hope of winning a jackpot one day kept me going. I knew I will get my father back on the day I won the lottery. This hope prompted me every Sunday to buy the ticket for him.

Sixteen years have passed since my father left and in these sixteen years, I have hardly talked to my mother. And whenever I have done so, I have deliberately tried to hurt her to make her feel guilty for my father. How can she live peacefully when I am yearning for my father?

The day, when I got my first job last year after completing my Masters, came as a fresh breath of air in my life. I was on cloud nine as I was able to maintain myself now and was free to move anywhere. I was just waiting to win the jackpot, which was the ticket to my father's heart.

It was a cold winter night when I was watching my favourite program on the TV and the doorbell rang. I opened the door and found my mother looking at me with an expression unknown to me. Suddenly she held my face in her hands and said, "Today I am free and am very happy for that. Free to live a life with my baby that I have always longed for." I noticed teardrops shining at the corners of her eyes and became speechless. I was absolutely clueless of what to say at that moment and stood in front of her, dumb, chewing my nails. She had taken voluntary retirement from her job.

After her retirement, I became the axis of her life around which her whole world was revolving. But perhaps it was too late now. The fact that she could have made my father stay back, never allowed me to be normal to her. I was sure her indifferent attitude had driven him out. I couldn't remember a single moment spent with her that can be cherished.

Engrossed in my thoughts, I was walking hurriedly to reach the market on time. Several questions were disturbing me. "Will I ever win the jackpot? Will I ever get the chance to go and live with my father?" It was my aim in life to gift the jackpot to my father and desperately wanted to win one. I was sure my father would accept me into his life after I win the prize.

After buying the ticket, I rushed to home as my mother had to leave to her sister's place. She was going to see her sister who was not well.

I took a sigh of relief when my mother left after lunch. Now I could spend the rest of the day in peace without getting disturbed by her presence in the house. It was a lovely day and I went to the backyard with a book in my hand. I was moving in the garden enjoying the beauty of the fresh blooms when suddenly my eyes fell on an old cupboard kept there…it was in a very bad condition. Wanting to have a closer look, I opened it and a small old diary slipped out of it. A thousand questions struck my mind in a flash of a moment. I wondered what could have been written in this diary. Unable to hold my curiosity, I bent and I picked it up. A small shriek came out of my mouth when I slowly opened it. It was my mother's diary that contained daily journals with every word written neatly and carefully in her handwriting. For a moment I hesitated, but the curiosity to read about her overtook every manner and etiquette of mine.

Clinching the diary to my chest, I came upstairs to my room and sat on a chair that was kept in the corner. Slowly with trembling hands, I opened it and started reading.

29th September 1998

Piyush, you can't imagine how eager I was today to go to the market with you and Khushi but wonder why you refused to take me with you. You always give me the excuse that dinner will not get ready on time if I go with you both. But you know today I had finished everything immediately after coming back from my office so I can spend some time with both of you. Still you didn't take me with you. I long for these small joyful moments with both of you but every time you have a new excuse ready. Hope Khushi enjoys her outing with you; love you both.

I was startled. Slowly I turned a few pages:

12th January 1999

Today, I came to know that you never wanted to marry me.

You wanted to get married to your classmate who was from a different caste but your family didn't allow you to. You had to marry me under their pressure and precisely this is the reason why you do not involve me in anything or take me anywhere with you and Khushi. You know I am a self-respecting woman and will never beg to you for what is rightfully mine. I know you are driving Khushi away from me and she has started avoiding me. But I am sure she will understand me when she grows up. After all she is my baby and all the more a woman.

I was stunned and couldn't believe what was written in the diary. Quickly I turned a few more pages:

18th June 1999

Your behaviour is overbearing for me. I feel so suffocated and humiliated with you. I would have left you long back but it is only Khushi who is holding me back. Her innocent face and my worries about her future have put an anchor in me; else the day you introduced me to your old classmate would have been my last day in this house. I know you meet her frequently and are still in contact with her.

15th September 1999

Ma is no more and with her all the restrictions on you to marry your classmate have perished. I know you have never been happy with us. Khushi was also just a tool for you who kept you away from me. You will never understand the meaning of the word

LOVE. She is a kid and can't differentiate between love and a convenient arrangement. But when she grows up, she will very easily gauge that the time you spend with her is not out of love but it is just a convenient arrangement that keeps you away from me. Till now I stayed with you for my baby, and today for her sake only I ask for a favour from you for the first and perhaps the last time in my life. Let's get divorced. I want her to be a strong person and don't want her to get shattered when she learns about your real feelings towards her.

12th January 2000

Today Khushi asked me to take her out. How can I explain, I have to take care of so many things alone that it becomes impossible for me to devote time for her. Now she is my responsibility alone and I need to take every measure to secure her future.

31st May 2014

I am so happy today. I have taken voluntary retirement and am free from my official duties. Now each and every moment of my life is for my baby, Khushi. I could never give her enough time due to my responsibilities. But now when she has got a job and is now self-sufficient, I can afford to leave my job and spend time with her to live the life I have always wished for. I know she needs some time to open up with me and I am ready to give her that time. Deep in my heart I know that she loves me.

My whole body was shaking like a leaf and I did not realise when tears started rolling from my eyes, covering my face. Throughout my life I had loved to hate my mother and never missed a chance to humiliate her. But every time she would give me a sad look and keep quiet. My life revolved only around two things: first was to humiliate my mother and the second to win a lottery to gift my father. But it seemed a storm had passed in front of me in the past couple of hours, changing the whole philosophy of my life. I don't know for how long I kept sitting there with tears rolling down my cheeks. The storm had passed and now everything was clear in front of me, like a clear sky after the pouring rain. The pages of the diary were fluttering in front of me and seemed to ridicule me for wasting so many precious years in hating my mom.

Suddenly the silence of the room was broken by ringing of the phone. I picked the receiver and a sweet voice fell into my ears, "ma'am, I am calling from the weekly lucky draw agency. You have won the third prize worth 100,000 rupees. You may collect your prize money from our counter anytime by showing your ticket and ID proof."

I felt like dancing with joy. So what if it was not the jackpot but it was the prize for which I had longed for all my life. But then I realised I no longer required the prize. What could be more ironical than the fact that all these years I longed to win to get the key to my father's heart and life and now that I had the key, I no longer needed it. The lock for which I was struggling to get the key had rusted.

The room had become dark and stuffy. I slowly got up and pulled the window curtains and golden rays of the evening sun filled the whole room with its radiance. I felt as if the rays were travelling through my heart, filling me with a fresh energy. An unknown happiness sprouted in me and in the bright sunlight, everything became clear to me.

I had wasted twenty four precious years in hating my mom but now it was time to make up for everything. With a pledge to fill her life with happiness, I decided to start by cooking her favourite dish for dinner. I could not wait to see the sparkle in her eyes when she would see the dinner prepared by me for her. But now the real test had started. I had never cared to know about my mom's favourite food, likes or dislikes. I have always seen her cooking my favourite dishes and doing things that I like. After scratching my head for long, I finally decided to cook something that was my favourite because I knew my mom would definitely like it. She had already prepared the dinner before leaving but I wanted to surprise her.

After buying some fresh vegetables and packs of noodles from the market, I collected my prize money and entered a sari shop. It was a big challenge for me to choose the colour of the sari as I was not aware of my mother's favourite colour. Sitting in front of a pile of colourful saris, I could see her smiling face in every piece that the salesman unfurled in front of me. Finally I chose a beautiful blue silk sari with thin *zari* border that gave it an elegant look. I headed towards the jeweller's shop after buying the sari, holding it tight against my chest in a jute bag.

Choosing a suitable piece of jewellery was no easier a task than buying the sari. The salesgirl displayed all kinds of jewellery in front of me but nothing seemed suitable for my mom. After struggling for long, when the sales girl showed me a pair of lovely tops studded with diamonds, I knew these were the ones for my mom. When I stepped out of the shop, a sense of deep satisfaction filled me. Feeling like the richest person in the world, I held both the packets tightly and strode towards home.

On my return, I started preparing the meal to get it ready before my mom arrived. I wanted to put all my love for twenty four years in it. By the time the shezwan noodles and chilli chicken were ready, it was quarter to nine. I kept the food in the hot cases and switched on the TV.

Time appeared to creep along at a snail's pace and when after a long wait I looked up at the clock, it was only ten minutes to nine. Finally somehow the wait was over and I ran to open the door when the doorbell rang. I stepped out and hug my mom tightly and started crying profusely. For a moment she stood there like a statue, surprised, and then hugged me back as tears rolled down her cheeks. After the initial burst of emotions settled, we went in and I took out the packets. My mother looked at me with questioning eyes.

"Mom, these are my gifts for you," I said.

While holding the packets, her hands were shaking and eyes were gleaming with a sparkle. Her eyes became wet when she opened the packet. This was the first ever gift that I had ever given her.

"These are lovely...the best gifts ever in my life," she said when she saw them. Her eyes were twinkling with pride and joy. I started pestering her to wear the sari and the tops at that very moment. Initially she hesitated a bit but later surrendered to my wish. When she stood before me in the blue silk sari and diamond studs, she appeared to be the most beautiful woman in the world. Her face was glowing with joy, pride and satisfaction, brighter than the diamonds she wore.

And that was the moment when I realised – I have won my jackpot. The jackpot after which I was running throughout my life, the jackpot that was supposed to change my life, was in front of me. My mom who is my world was right in front of me, always, and I was running after a mirage, something that never existed.

Story 12: Destiny

When I reached the platform, the train had already arrived and only five minutes were left for it to leave the station. Every entrance of the train was overflowing with flocks of passengers who were trying to make their way to their respective compartments before it started. Hawkers were also trying their luck by squeezing in between the passengers and attracting their attention with their much-rehearsed sales pitch, hoping to make some last minute sales.

Hurrying through the sea of people, I followed the coolie, making my way towards the train. Every compartment was full with all kinds of passengers, who were busy settling down on their respective berths. The corridors were packed with the trolleys, baskets, bags and all types of luggage that were obstructing the paths of the passengers with their presence. Hopping over these obstacles and clearing every hurdle on my way, when I managed to reach my designated seat, the train had already started moving after announcing its departure with a screeching whistle.

As the train was picking up speed, a young man in his mid-twenties jumped on it and entered the coupe where I was sitting. By looking at his pair of blue branded jeans, grey jacket, a neatly done hairdo and the elitist look in his eyes behind a pair of expensive glasses, it was apparent that he belonged to a well-to-do family. He occupied the seat beside me and taking out a file from his bag, started checking some papers kept in it. "May be a fresh entrant in a job," I thought to myself.

By this time, I had also settled at my place and with the intention of learning some more about those with whom I had to spend the next eighteen hours, I glanced at the other co-passengers sitting in the compartment.

The side berth was occupied by a couple with a small child. The wife took out a women's magazine from her bag and started flipping the pages while the husband made his daughter sit on his lap and was showing her everything through the window that passed the train...the fields, the trees, cows grazing on the fields and huts that appeared like tiny toy houses from the distance. The child was gazing at the scenery outside, which kept changing with every moment and started clapping with joy whenever she caught sight of anything that appeared interesting to her.

I moved my sight from the small girl to the two middle-aged gentlemen who were sitting at the opposite berth. One of them wore a pair of spectacles and bore a strange look in his eyes that seemed to have the capacity to take an X-ray of any person he looked at. Feeling somewhat uncomfortable by the strange look in his eyes, I quickly removed my eyes from him and fixed it at his neighbour who was trying to prove some point very aggressively by thumping his fist on the berth. They were perhaps discussing about the latest step taken by the government to make some amendments in the current education system and happened to be supporters of two different parties, which had brought in such heat to the discussion.

The *Outlook* magazine that I had managed to buy from the hawker while boarding the train was lying on my lap while I quietly listened to their discussion. Their intense discussion came to a halt when the catering people came to serve us the evening tea. Coming to terms with the world, one of the gentlemen looked at me and exchanged a smile.

Turning towards the young man who was still engrossed in his file, he asked, "Are you going on an official tour?"

"Nope!" the young man looked up and said. "Going to appear for an interview," and again buried his face in the file.

By now we all had served ourselves the tea and indulged in some chitchat when suddenly the gentleman with the spectacles asked me, "If I am not wrong then you are associated with banking industry." For a moment, the cup I was holding in my hand shook, but I controlled it to prevent the tea spilling from it. Surprised, I replied with another question, "But how did you know?"

"Well, I can read faces and the lines of forehead and your face is telling me that you are going to leave your job soon."

"This is simply amazing!" I said. "I am planning to set up a business of my own and am going to Delhi in the same context."

Our conversation had attracted many and several heads turned towards us to listen to it. The other person who was busy talking to this gentleman earlier joined us and said in a sarcastic tone, "I don't believe in all these things. You know a palmist told me during my college days that I would never get a job." He smiled a meaningful smile and paused for a moment to say again, "Now can anyone tell me what the hell I have been doing for the past twenty one years?"

"It's all about belief. Moreover it also depends on the competency of the reader," came the expert comment from the person sitting at the side berth. By now the discussion was charged up and everyone had jumped in to narrate his or her opinion and experiences on the topic. I noticed the young man had kept his file aside and was listening to the discussion very seriously. After a few moments he extended his hand towards the gentleman who claimed to read forehead and said, "Can you please tell me something about my interview? Will I get this job?"

The gentleman laughed, "I read faces and forehead my dear friend, not palms."

"Then please read my face and give me the answer of my question?"

The gentleman slid towards the edge of his seat and looked very intently at the young man's face. Already convinced about his knowledge in the subject by whatever he had told me, I was curious to know what he says about the young man. Everyone was looking at him, waiting to listen what he says.

Suddenly the gentleman started sweating profusely. Unlikely in the month of December when whole of Northern India was struggling with the deadly cold wave, his sweating left all of us surprised.

"What happened? Is everything okay?" asked the other fellow co-passenger sitting beside him.

"Yes, I am fine," he said taking out a handkerchief from his pocket and wiped the beads of sweat from his forehead contradicting his own statement. His condition was getting worse which was evident by his shaking hands and the nervousness that had covered his face.

"Does anybody have a first aid box?" I asked looking at everyone sitting in the compartment. Everyone nodded in negative.

"I am fine," the person repeated. His eyes were fixed on the young man and it was very difficult to gauge at that moment which expression dominated the looks in his eyes that was a mix of nervousness, sympathy, anxiety and confusion.

The young man got up with a jolt and brushing the crease of his jacket said, "Let me find out from the other passengers if they have a first aid box."

As soon as he left the coupe, the gentleman got up from his seat and started walking back and forth on the passage between the two berths, repeating the words, "This can't be true. How is it possible?"

We all were completely clueless about the reason behind the man's sudden restlessness as he had been otherwise perfectly fine a few moments back.

"Why don't you sit down for a while till the first aid box arrives?" the other middle-aged gentleman said.

"It will never arrive and I also know the reason why," the man said and banged the wall with his fist.

"But that fellow has gone to bring help. You don't bother. Just a matter of couple of moments," the first passenger tried to soothe him.

"*That* fellow has gone to bring help and this is the reason why I said, the help will never arrive. And you know why?" he said, his words appearing to be coming from a distant location, cold with disappointment.

"Why," we all asked in chorus.

"Because he is destined to die today." It felt like someone had poured molten lead in our ears. "By this time he should have been on his heavenly journey. I am just a bit confused and nervous how he is still alive," he said in a whispering tone and sat with a thud on one of the berths.

There was pin-drop silence in the coupe. Only the rhythmic sound of the wheels moving on the tracks could be heard.

"And how do you know that?" I asked, trying to control my heart, which was now beating very fast, hoping to get a clue to gauge if this was any kind of prank on all of us.

"Didn't you see I was reading his forehead? It's written on it."

And then a long silence engulfed the coupe. We all were trying to come to terms with the situation when the noise from the adjacent compartment pierced through our compartment. The train started slowing down and came to a halt with a screeching sound from its brakes. Someone had pulled the chain. Hoping everything was fine, all of us rushed towards the door that had flung open and there was no sign of the young man.

We looked at the field outside where his body was lying on the ground, lifeless.

"Poor boy! He was enquiring about a first aid box from all of us. A sudden jerk and he fell straight out of the train. But it was not the jerk but destiny that pulled him to the ground," someone was saying from behind. The word "destiny" banged in my head like a hammer as I stared at the lifeless body. I felt as if someone whispered in my ears, "Destiny. He is destined to die today."

Story 13: The Untimely Death

"Ma where is my music notebook? I am getting late!" I shouted from my room while hurriedly putting my slippers on. Today I had two extra classes in my school

because of which I was late for my music tuition class. The half-yearly examinations were approaching and the teachers were completing their syllabi by taking extra classes. I hated it when I had to stay back after school hours. Moreover when the subject was social studies, I felt like jumping out from the window of the classroom and run back home. Extra classes also meant skipping my afternoon meal and hurrying for my music class; and today was one such day.

"What shall I do with this girl?" Ma came to my room, muttering, and handed me the notebook, which was lying at the corner of my study table.

Putting it in my bag, I rushed out and quickly climbed my bicycle. Humming the new song that I had learned in my music class, I peddled hard through the shortcut to reach there on time. Music is my life and I cannot imagine missing a class even in my wildest dreams. And today was a special day as my teacher had promised to teach us a new *shabad* for the forthcoming Guru Parab.

I have been learning Indian classical music from the age of five and took the tuitions from a renowned singer who incidentally happened to be the wife of one of our campus residents. My ma'am was totally dedicated towards music and never restricted herself from teaching us songs and bhajans outside the syllabus. So my *shabad* lessons were waiting for me and I was getting thrilled by the thought of singing it on Guru Nanak's Jayanti. Oh that reminds me, I forgot to tell you about the Gurudwara that was built few years back in our campus. It was a lovely small Gurudwara that shared its wall with one of the boundaries of the campus. I always liked its serene and pious atmosphere and loved to go there on Guru Nanak Dev's birthday every year when the whole campus gathered to celebrate the festival. The most awaited part of the festivity for me was the time when *langar* was distributed. Food from the most expensive restaurants cannot match the taste of the *kada prasad, puri and chane* that we got after the ceremony. This year another attraction made the celebration all the more worthwhile for me when my ma'am called me and said, "Shilpi, this year you will sing *shabad* with me on Guru Parab."

"Me?" I exclaimed with joy, unable to believe my ears. It was the most prestigious offer for any music student and after hearing the news I felt as if I have been awarded a trophy. The practice sessions had gone well and I was counting the days for the D-day when few days before the festival, the radio dropped a bomb on us with a news. Winter had already knocked on our doors and the weather was changing slowly. The hot dusty wind had turned into mild cool breeze and it felt nice to sit in the warm rays of sun to enjoy winter afternoons. One such afternoon, ma was knitting a sweater for me while sitting in the backyard and listening to the All India Radio when suddenly the newsreader said, "*Mrs Gandhi has been shot today morning by two of her bodyguards.*"

Ma dropped her knitting yarn and needles on the chair and ran towards the radio as if increasing the volume would change the announcer's mind and this time it would say, "I am sorry. Our news writer got confused and took today's date as 1st April. The inconvenience caused due to this poor joke is highly regretted." But alas! It was no joke and Mrs Gandhi was actually shot by her own bodyguards. Then started the series of news where every time the reader said the same thing, "*Prime Minister Indira Gandhi has been taken to All India Institute of Medical Sciences for medical attention and is under close observation of the doctors after a surgery.*"

One India-Pakistan cricket match had been abruptly cancelled midway, and we all huddled around the radio to get the news of the wellbeing of the prime minister. It was towards the evening when the Urdu bulletin transmitted via All India Radio reported the news of Mrs Gandhi's death.

When Baba came home, he found us all waiting for him at the main entrance. Shocked by the terrible news of the assassination of Mrs Gandhi, ma, my elder sister and I were waiting eagerly for him at the main door.

"Have you heard the news?" ma asked as soon as she caught sight of Baba. Baba was busy in a meeting in the office and did not know about the news. He was startled to learn about the tragedy and could not believe whatever had happened.

"Get me some money and the shopping bags," he said without even stepping into the house. Startled, we all looked at each other trying to make sense of the utterly confusing words said by him.

"What has happened to you? I am talking about the assassination of Mrs Gandhi," ma asked, a little irritated.

"Yes, I know very well. And I also know the after effects of such assassinations. Have you forgotten that I have seen what followed Mahatma Gandhi's assassination?"

He returned with bags full of grocery items and vegetables. And whatever he told us explained it all. He was anticipating the markets to be closed for the next couple of days as an after effect of the incident.

Soon to our horror, the whole nation turned into a burning cauldron after the disgraceful incident. Huge mobs, carrying rods and kerosene, looted shops and crushed humanity under their feet. Our school was closed for unknown period of time and winter vacations started much before they should have been. And why only our school? Every college and office was closed for an indefinite period of time after the riots got started. Violence broke out on the streets of the town and humanity was slaughtered bit by bit every moment. Frenzied mobs butchered and burnt thousands of Sikhs, alive, in the riots. The inhumanity was frightening. Even the children were not spared. Life within the campus had come to a standstill. The whole town was burning outside like hell but thanks to the communal harmony and maturity level of the people residing within the campus, it was untouched by any such kind of feeling or activity.

But some of our Sardar uncles removed their turbans and cut their hair short out of fear of the riots. Everyone, especially Hindus started feeling guilty for the step taken by them. No one had the courage to face them for something that they had not done.

Slowly and gradually the life started moving within the campus but the curfew was still on in the town outside. Eventually people felt the need of food and grocery, which was now going out of stock in every house. The tragedy broke on thirty-first and it was the last day of the month. Most of our neighbours had yet to do their monthly grocery shopping when the markets got closed for indefinite period of time. And thus started our little act of social service. Being the youngest in the house, it became my duty to distribute rice and flour along with some fresh raw vegetables in our neighbourhood. Thanks to Baba's presence of mind and ma's hobby of gardening that had given us a grand kitchen garden, it provided us ample fruits and vegetables of superior quality. Slowly and gradually many tiny shops that had cropped within the campus came to everyone's rescue. Farmers from nearby area started coming to sell their vegetables in the campus area and once again life within the campus started moving smoothly.

The beauty of life lies in its motion. It never stops for anything and so gradually everything started appearing normal. Schools reopened after a long unwarranted vacation and we all started trying to go back to our normal routine. Guru Parab had passed and so did my chance to sing in the ceremony. However, I was happy to join school again and it was my first day after the vacations. Winter was in its full bloom and Kanpur winters are so terrible that it leaves everyone shivering so hard that you feel like your teeth are going to fall off. But I was enjoying my day with my friends and did not mind the ruthless wrath of the weather amidst the warm presence of everyone.

I was going to attend my SUPW (Socially Useful Productive Work) class with my classmates when suddenly my eyes fell on my biology teacher. She was a real beauty and was famous among us girls for her outfits. Sweet natured and helpful, she was loved by all. And we girls? We all waited every day to have a glance of what she wore that day. Every sari that she wore was unique in its own way and her frequent visits to abroad had got her several extraordinarily beautiful winter wear. Our eyes were widened and jaws got dropped when we saw her wrapped in a thin shawl and wearing an old *salwar-kameez*. Oh let me tell you her name bore the surname "Kaur." So we quickly wished her and moved from the place, unable to bear the sight.

Eager to learn a new craft, when we entered the lab, we saw our ma'am seriously busy at something. It was a pleasant shock for us as we found our dear ma'am, who was always encouraging us by her scolding, quietly doing something. Mustering all the courage in our hearts, some of us went to her and asked for the new lesson. But whatever she said was enough to send us all to a state of shock. The whole family of our biology teacher was killed in the riot. The mob barged into their house and both of her brothers were slashed to death. Luckily she was in another town with her grandparents. But the rioters got hold of her father and pulled him to the top of the roof from where he was thrown alive in the fire that was burning on the streets. Later her house was set on fire that burnt everything they possessed. And this was the reason why our SUPW teacher was knitting a sweater on the automatic knitting machine for hers–she who had been a proud owner of loads of expensive sweaters, coats and jackets.

We did not know what to say. Words had lost their meaning behind the brutal dance of inhumanity. Pin-drop silence enveloped the whole class. Only the sound of the panels running over the machine could be heard and we all stared at ma'am with moist eyes, as she quietly knit the sweater.

All the fizz of joining school and meeting friends after so many days died down after the incident. Somehow the day got over and I climbed my bicycle to return home. Today I had no music class so there was no hurry and I was riding via the main route. When I neared the Gurudwara, my heart started beating very fast. Although the campus was free from any riot or communal disharmony, the Gurudwara was closed for all times to come, which meant no more Guru Parab celebrations and no more *shabads*. Above all, this meant no more annual gathering of people from all communities to celebrate the festival. I looked at the huge iron lock hanging at the gate of the Gurudwara and a deep sigh came out of my mouth.

A beautiful relationship had died an untimely death.

Story 14: Before It's Too Late

Before Arnab could realise it, life had changed for him. Having dinner with family changed into late night strategy workshops. Weekly outings turned into business meetings. Sweet and short chats on phone calls during lunchtime with his wife transformed into hour long teleconferences. Spending time with kids in the evening doing nothing tangible seemed meaningless–he would lose at least an hour in the bargain that could be well invested in completing the office presentation. Overall there was no respite from the hectic office and future planning.

Arnab had come a long way from the lower middle class lifestyle that had shaped his childhood. Now when he is a part of the sophisticated upper middle class society and living the dream that didn't allow him to sleep throughout his student life, he seldom found any time to spend with his family. Arnab, boasting of his new Atlas cycle and flaunting it in front of his friends, is now unknown to the Arnab who owns one Mercedes Benz, one Innova and one Skoda Octavia.

Life had showered mercy with both the hands on Arnab and today he enjoys the citizenship of the upper strata of the society. His eyes shine with a sense of pride when Sharmila leaves in her expensive saris for her NGO that is engaged in social work for downtrodden children. So what if he could not afford to have an entry-level mobile phone during the early days of his career? His chest swells in pride when he sees Ravi spending hours with his latest gadgets.

Life was moving smoothly, happy and content when an article in the newspaper acted as an atom bomb that dropped on Arnab. There was nothing special in the morning that started with the same old routine but ended with a life changing realisation for him. "Live before you die"–the words written in the article got carved into his mind.

"What am I gaining among all this bustle?" the thought that he had sedated very carefully in the morning, again rose in his mind troubling him while driving home in the night. "The day passes in meetings, conferences and strategy formulations. By the time I reach home, everyone is asleep. I hardly get any time to spend with those who mean the world to me."

Arnab looked at the mirror and noticed a patch of white hair above his ears. "I have earned enough for a lifetime. Now it's time to enjoy with family," he thought and felt as if someone had opened the doors of the cage that was holding him through all these years. A smile appeared on his face as he felt as though he was flying over cloud nine–light and happy. By the time he reached home a concrete decision had taken shape in his mind.

Next day when Arnab opened his sleepy eyes, he saw Sharmila standing at his bedside, asking him to get up. "Are you not feeling well? It's already seven."

"I am on leave today." Saying this, he smiled and got up, sitting at the edge of the bed, swinging his legs.

"On WHAT?" Sharmila asked, unable to decipher the meaning of this long-heard word. But by now Arnab had already entered the washroom and bolted it from inside, leaving Sharmila alone with the mystery to be solved by herself.

Sharmila couldn't decide which feeling possessed her more: amazement or confusion. She sat still at the corner of the bed for a couple of moments but then postponing the job of finding out the reason behind Arnab's leave, she went to the kitchen to instruct the cook to prepare Arnab's favourite breakfast. When Arnab entered the dining room after taking a shower, the aroma of freshly prepared *aloo parathas* had filled the whole atmosphere. Elated with the sight of hot *aloo parathas* inviting him with their aroma, Arnab asked Sharmila who was waiting for him at the table, "When was the last time we had *aloo paratha* for breakfast?"

"Well, I think you should ask *when was the last time we had breakfast together* instead," Sharmila chuckled.

"Where is Ravi?" he asked pulling a chair for himself.

"Sleeping."

"So late?"

"Yes his college starts at eleven in the morning," Sharmila said putting a *paratha* on the plate kept in front of Arnab. Everything seemed so alien to Arnab; he felt as though he was living somebody else's life.

"Now tell me what is the plan," Sharmila, unable to bear the tension of the suspense, finally asked him.

"No plans at all. I am leaving my job," Arnab said coolly, putting a piece of *aloo paratha* in his mouth after dipping it into thick creamy yoghurt.

"What?" Sharmila felt as if someone has pushed her from the top floor of the multi-storey building of the society flats they were living in.

"Yes, I will be working as a consultant now."

The *parathas* turned bitter, losing their taste in Sharmila's mouth. She poured herself a glass of water and drank it down in one gulp.

"Shall we go for a movie today? We'll also have lunch outside," unaware of what Sharmila was going through at the moment, Arnab continued in his own enthusiasm. His eyes were glowing with the same excitement that they bore when he was a child and he got half an hour extra from his mother to play cricket with his friends.

But words seemed to coming from a far off distance for Sharmila. She was lost in her own world of friends, 'social work' and kitty party while her mind wandered thinking about the ridicule she will have to face in front of her kitty friends. How is she going to introduce herself now? "Hi, I am Sharmila. My husband works as a *Consultant*?" The mere thought was enough to make her feel miserable.

"Hey! Are you listening?" Arnab who was looking at Sharmila with anticipation, asked her after a few moments of silence on not getting any response from her.

"I would have loved to dear," coming to terms, Sharmila said with a faint smile and continued, "...but I have to attend a meeting for the NGO I am associated with."

Almost instantaneously, the glow on Arnab's face vanished and it turned greyish-white.

"Can't you postpone it for one day? As it is you are not directly associated with it. You pay only occasional visits to the organisation."

"Yes, but after that I have a kitty party with my friends which was planned more than a week ago. I am sorry can't make it today," she said. "But don't mind dear! We will definitely go for the movie next week. This week is fully packed." Sharmila quickly got up from the dining table and went inside to get ready. She did not want Arnab to notice her restlessness on his decision of leaving his job. The brimming enthusiasm on Arnab's face vanished. He picked up the newspaper and opened to read it.

The clock had already struck ten and Ravi was still in his bed. Sharmila had left for her 'social work' and Arnab, trying to figure out his routine for the day, was waiting for Ravi to get up. When he came out of his room, he was all ready for the college.

"Hey Dad! What a pleasant surprise," Ravi rejoiced as he saw Arnab who was still reading the newspaper. After reading every word of the newspaper, he was now reading the editorial. "Didn't go to office today?"

"I am on leave," Arnab replied.

"Oh okay."

"So, what are your plans for today?" Arnab smiled and asked.

"Nothing special Dad! As usual. First college, then some outings with friends," he replied.

Ravi's innocent face, when he was a kid, flashed in Arnab's mind. Every Sunday he used to ask Arnab while putting his arms around his neck to take him for an outing. But those were the years when Arnab was busy securing his and his family's future. Every time Arnab used to pacify him with a promise of great outing together sometime in future. But throughout these years, he never got the opportunity to go out with him. Today, he thought, was the time to make up for the loss.

"Shall we both go for the outing today? Only two of us? We will have lots of fun together," Arnab asked with great expectation putting his hand around Ravi's shoulders.

"Eh? Oh come on Dad! Our likes and dislikes are very different. We'll feel bored in each other's company," Ravi said instantly. "Moreover I have already promised my friends. It's better you go with Mom," he suggested and picked up the keys of his car to go.

"Love you Dad! See ya!" he said and went out waving his hands.

"Breakfast?" Arnab wanted to say but the words died in his mouth. For how long he kept sitting there staring the path through which Ravi left, Arnab himself didn't know. He felt a sinking feeling inside him. Nothing was happening as imagined. He was not prepared for such a lukewarm response from his family.

"Why don't you take another job?" Sharmila used to say. "This job is not only costing us our lives but it's costing you your health as well!"

"All this is for our future dear," he used to console her. "Once we save enough for us, I'll leave my job."

"I will be waiting for that day," used to be her reply. But when *that* day had finally arrived, no one seemed to be excited. Everyone was busy in his or her life. And among all this business, Arnab felt life has progressed, leaving him far behind.

In the process of winning the race of life, he had forgotten the basic rule of living. You have to catch the spring before it's too late. You cannot expect the freshness and aroma from a flower after it has dried. A dried flower ceases to spread fragrance.

Arnab's life had also dried. He wanted to hold the moments to live them later but he forgot that moments are like butterflies. They fly everywhere but you cannot catch them. You can live the moments, enjoy them; but if you try to hold them, they slip out of your hands. But it was too late for him to realise this.

Heaving a sigh of resentment, he got up and started getting ready. It was only eleven. If he hurried, he could easily attend the meeting to be held at 12:30 pm.

Story 15: The Sealed Wish

Martha's eyes are glued to the urn kept on the bookrack while her hands move swiftly like a professional chef over the chopping board. Her constant gaze is initially directed towards the beautiful motifs carved on the surface of the urn but later she starts visualising, in her mind, various things that could have been stored within the sealed copper urn, which has been lying majestically on her bookrack for the past couple of weeks. She has not been able to sleep even for a single night, ever since she brought the urn home.

Though, now, sleepless nights have become her regular companion from the day since she lost her daughter, Christine, in a maddening crowd five years back. The incident is still fresh in her memory and images of people running and shouting crazily still haunt her, giving her chills that freeze her spine. Whenever her daughter's innocent face floats in front of her eyes, she gets drenched in a stream of sweat and it seems like someone is squeezing her chest hard, pricking a thousand needles into it. Her life is confined within the four walls of the house where she wanders alone, recalling every moment spent with Christine. The day passes with the small kids, teaching them the alphabet and colours in school, but the nights are unbearable. Ever since Martha has brought the urn home, she has even lost the occasional sleep she managed to get amidst the entire internal turmoil that she has been undergoing for the past couple of years. She waits for the night to pass, listening to the ticking of the clock hanging on the wall, which echoes like a drum beat in the quietness that prevails through stillness of the night.

An unknown force seems to be drawing her towards the urn, requesting to unveil the mystery behind its occupant. With every passing day, Martha gets all the more engrossed in the thoughts of the small piece of antique art guessing the names of things that could be residing quietly in it. The only silver lining in all this chaos is the fact that now she has some escape from the pain she has been experiencing since she lost Christine. The squeezing pain that she felt in her chest has now diminished and has been taken over by an unknown quest to find the answer behind the sealed urn.

Christine was only three years old when Martha lost her in the dreadful incident. After getting a divorce from David, Martha's world revolved around Christine. Her eyes sparkled with happiness and face gleamed with love whenever she listened to Christine's chirpy voice and laughter. A certain amount of pride filled her when her little daughter came running and said, "Mom, I love you. You are the best." Christine's hair, a rich shade of golden, flowed in waves to adorn her glowing, porcelain-like skin. Her glistening chestnut brown eyes framed by long lashes were bright and they seemed to brighten the world with the happiness they bore. With her straight nose and pink lips she seemed to be the most beautiful creation God had ever made. When she smiled, Martha would sigh with contentment. When she laughed, Martha would laugh with her. And when she wept, it seemed to Martha that she would be swept away in a sea of tears.

It seems to have happened yesterday, when Martha decided to take Christine to the summer festival being celebrated in London. She would do anything to see a smile on Christine's face and these festivals made her crazy, especially when she got the chance to be a part of all the fun, ride various types of rides and see a colourful world entirely unknown in the small town of England where she lived with Martha. When they reached the venue on the black Sunday afternoon, the festival was alive with the laughter of children and women, moving from one stall to another looking for the things they could buy now and cherish later. There was a smile on the face of every man, looking happy and content as they witnessed the joy of their family members. Martha and Christine also became a part of this festivity and were enjoying every moment of it when suddenly the whole atmosphere got filled with the screams of people. There was sight of people running in every direction and they were calling out to their family members who had got separated. Trying to understand what was happening, Martha looked around the whole ground, horrified. All she could see was a sea of people running and screaming, horrified. She looked to her left and found a huge ball of fire. Its violent and impetuous flames were engulfing everything that came into its contact. She quickly held the hands of little Christine and ran towards the exit and the shock of her life struck her.

"I want to go to Mom. Please take me to her," someone cried.

Martha looked down and froze when she saw that it was not Christine but a small boy who was standing there, holding her hands, crying for his mother. Immediately, two wet chestnut brown eyes, eager to find her mother in the huge crowd, danced in front of her eyes. "Christine, my dear! Where are you?" she cried out loud. She searched the whole ground, she screamed, she called her name several times but everything proved to be worthless. It seemed as if Christine had vanished into thin air.

Since then Martha has been going through hell and every passing moment seems like a curse to her. Every effort to find her little daughter has filled her with more anguish and a void has begun to grow with every passing day. In these five years, the sounds of people shouting and running all over the ground have continued to haunt her. The baffled yells of running people and wagons still echo in her mind and every night she gets up with a jolt on the bed.

This is the first time she is thinking about something else than Christine. The spectacular urn, that made a dramatic entry in Martha's life, has given her a reason to look forward. She has got a reason to get up every morning, when the urge to find out what is inside the urn fills her with a certain kind of excitement.

It was the beauty of this antique urn that drew her towards it. She had walked like a hypnotised person towards the lady selling this urn, amazed by the charm of the antique piece. She had brought the urn home, few days back, on a lazy Sunday afternoon. After finishing all household chores, there was nothing much significant left for her to do that could qualify as 'urgent' or 'important.' To pass some time and divert her thoughts from Christine, she switched on the TV, hoping to find some interesting programs on it, only to be disappointed with the same old daily soaps trying to amuse the audience with their over-dramatised melodramatic acts.

She went to the bookshelf and scanned the rack but all the books kept on it had their share of the journey with the reader more than once. She picked up a book randomly and looked out of the window, at the bright sunny afternoon and the colourful flowers that were in full bloom giving a cheerful ambience to the whole landscape. She gazed at the kids who were honing their skating skills on the concrete road, making way for other kids who were enjoying bicycle riding.

She stood in front of the window for a while, watching the kids playing, when the ice cream van announced its arrival by playing the tinkling song it played every day. She looked up at the clock that showed 3 pm. "One can even set the time with this music," she thought and a faint smile flashed on her lips. Two to three kids ran inside their houses to bring money to buy ice cream from this local vendor.

The happy and gay atmosphere outside enveloped her for a couple of moments and the idea of having a visit to the market struck her. Maybe the hustle and bustle of the car boot sale that happened to be organised every Sunday in the open area or parking of the local market could relieve her from the agony for a while. At least she can spend a few hours scanning through the interesting items being sold at the sale. These sales were her favourites. She was a frequent visitor to these, where people gather to sell old items that they bring in their cars to sell and display them in their car boots. Maybe this will distract her thoughts from her loss for a couple of hours. Quickly picking up her wallet and the car keys, she moved out of the house.

"Hello, Ms Martha," greeted two kids, who were buying ice cream from the vendor. "Hello," she said and smiled back while starting the car. It hardly took her five minutes to reach the market. A galore of homeless items was waiting in the car boots for people to provide them a new home. Moving from one boot to other, Martha examined every item. Jewellery, videos, books, clothes, toys, garden pots, small kitchen appliances, vases…nothing aroused her interest. She went around the whole area and was turning to come back when her eyes spotted something interesting. It was an old copper urn. Well antique would be the right term as the urn possessed all the qualities that could earn it the title 'antique.' Engraved with beautiful floral motifs, this urn was about one foot tall, fit to enjoy a place in a Maharaja's palace. She halted, with sparkles in her eyes, and picked it up to see the label on it. '£30' it read.

The price was HUGE considering the fact that it was an old urn being sold at the boot sale of a small town in the UK. But Martha's connoisseur vision about antiques assured her that the deal would be a profitable one.

"Hello, may I have the keys please?" she asked the lady selling the urn, pointing towards the locked clasps of the urn. There seemed to be something inside the urn as it weighed more than a normal empty urn. The lady reached out to Martha after returning some balance change to another customer and said a little hesitantly, "I am sorry but I don't have its keys either."

"But how? You must have the keys if you locked it?" Martha asked in a confused tone.

"Recently, I bought a house along with its belongings. I found this urn in the garage while cleaning it before I moved in. So have no clues about the keys."

Trying to solve the mystery of what the urn could have been storing, Martha gave another glance to the urn. It was too beautiful to be left just for the sake of the locked clasps. She reached out to her wallet and paid for the urn. Since then, two weeks had passed, but Martha was unable to drift her thoughts from the urn.

Days had been passing with the same monotony when suddenly the lady who sold her the urn appeared again to turn her world upside down. The school where she taught had reopened after summer break and she was returning home after another hectic day when she was startled to see the lady at the gate of the school.

"Hello! What brings you here and how did you know I teach in this school?" Martha asked, a little puzzled.

"My grandson studies in this school and I have seen you here couple of times. Found this the other day while looking for a tool in the toolbox. Maybe this can help you with the urn." The lady stretched her palm where a small key lied quietly.

"Thank you!" Martha said picking up the key, elated to be able to find the answer to the question that kept her awake for so many days. Her face glowed with a radiance of remarkable joy and her heartbeats started racing.

Taking the keys from the lady, Martha strode towards her home unable to stay there for another moment. The past few days had been highly torturous. And today finally her wait would be over. Unlocking the door with trembling hands, she threw her purse on the sofa and rushed towards the bookrack. Click. The key went in and Martha was dumbstruck for a moment. It seemed as if someone had pushed her from the top of a cliff. The most bizarre truth awaited inside the urn for Martha that made her dumb for few minutes.

Somebody's cremated remains in the form of ashes filled the urn to its brim. When the initial flabbergasted feeling faded a bit, Martha was filled with deep anguish and disgust. Who in the world could have left the ashes of a near and dear one in the urn? She wondered. She had read somewhere that Indians keep the ashes of the departed in such urns before the final ritual… but why would anybody keep it here?

"I must find out whose ashes are these. They deserve a fitting destination," she thought to herself. On the third day of her wait for the lady at her school gate, she saw her coming to pick her grandson. Martha's quest for truth started after taking the address of the previous owner of the house from the lady.

The house was sold by a lady who now lives in Birmingham. Throughout her drive to Birmingham, she felt something churning inside her stomach. Thanking her stars about getting such an early appointment from the lady, when Martha reached the house, it was already noon. The excitement that she felt all the while vanished into thin air and a sinking feeling started gripping her with the sight of the house. Unsure of what would be the outcome of the meeting, Martha rang the doorbell.

An Indian lady in her mid-thirties opened the door. She looked confident yet relaxed in her light blue T-shirt and black jeans. But deep in her eyes there was a void that appeared to be very familiar to Martha. After greeting Martha, she invited her in.

"Hello! I am Neha. Please come in," she said in a soft voice.

"I am sorry I bothered you at such an hour on Sunday. You probably have some plans for the day," Martha said while settling down on the huge sofa kept in the corner of the room.

"It's perfectly alright," she said in a soft tone. "What brings you here? How can I help you?"

"Recently I bought this urn in a garage sale from a lady who has bought your home at Ashton," she said taking out the picture of the urn from her handbag and extending it towards Neha. Neha's eyes became moist as she took the photograph from Martha. "This urn is filled with someone's ashes and I want to know the name of the person whose remains are kept in it. I thought you might know about it," she said again.

"These are Abha, my niece's, ashes," Neha said as a teardrop dropped on the photograph escaping her eyes.

"My brother and sister-in-law had christened her *Abha* meaning *glow* because they believed she had filled their childless life with happiness. Last year Abha was diagnosed with late stage cancer and lost the battle in eight months. No medicines or treatment could save her." She paused for a while and looked at Martha's face who was now looking at her without blinking. "My brother and sister-in-law wanted to scatter her ashes in the Ganges in India, as it is said that immersing last remains in the river gets you salvation," she continued. "They were returning after doing the final shopping to leave for India when they joined their loving daughter after meeting with an accident."

Neha lifted the glass of water from the table and took a sip to clear her choking throat and said, "I did not agree with them because Abha was not Indian by birth. She was a British girl who was adopted by my brother and sister-in-law five years back, and I believed she deserved her last rites to be performed as per the customs Christians follow."

"British…five years back…adopted…" The words rang like knell in Martha's head and small droplets of sweat started building up on her forehead.

"Precisely why I left the urn with other belongings in the house when I sold it to the British lady. I was sure sooner or later she will find it and provide Abha a suitable farewell," Neha sighed.

"Do you have a photograph of your niece?" Martha asked in a shaking voice and her heart started beating so fast, she feared it will leap out of her body.

"Yes, please wait for a moment. I'll just come," Neha said, getting up to go inside. Martha kept sitting there, praying silently. It appeared to her as if ages had passed since Neha went inside. When Neha entered the room again, there was a photo album in her hand. Sitting beside Martha, she opened the album and showed her a photograph.

Martha felt her world was coming crashing down. She tried to look at the photograph with her wet eyes but everything started getting hazy. She rubbed her eyes with her hands and tried again. Five years later, the familiar chestnut brown eyes were staring at Martha poignantly.